"Young Grey is jealous. I think your game is fairly won."

"Stop it! Don't make it sound so calculating, and besides...I don't know if my 'game,' as you put it, is the same as it was a few weeks ago."

His eyes were intent on her own. "Just what are you holding out for?"

"'Tis simple, my lord, and you are answered in one word: love."

He had her soundly in his arms. There was no holding himself back any more. A guttural release, scarcely audible: "Damn!"

She discovered his grip was binding and tantalizing. She was responding to a kiss fiery with passion, and then she felt herself flung away.

MARY, SWEET MARY

Claudette Williams

FAWCETT CREST • NEW YORK

A Fawcett Crest Book
Published by Ballantine Books
Copyright © 1980 by Claudette Williams

ISBN 0-449-21541-5

Manufactured in the United States of America

First Fawcett Coventry Edition: September 1980
First Ballantine Books Edition: April 1988

*Dedicated with love to
my new sister, Diane.*

Chapter One

Dark eyes opened wide. Rosy lips pursed. A white, delicate hand fluttered to move but was held back in self-control as a petite figure sat back and awaited the outcome of the discussion at hand. Mary of Montlaine knew that if anyone could sway her brother, it was his wife, Vanessa, Lady Montlaine, and thus she kept silent even though it was her future at stake.

"Bother!" Vanessa stamped, and her gray eyes glittered defiantly. "You can't mean to stand here and argue with me, my lord."

Her husband's dark, dark eyes grew stormy, yet behind their depths lurked his ever-silent admiration. "I don't mean to do anything of the kind. Mary shall accompany us home to Montlaine, and that, my love, is that."

"Oh? Is it, do you think?" Vanessa's hands threw a wayward auburn curl over her shoulder. She was about to rant at him and then suddenly bethought another mode of behavior might serve.

She took a turn in place, and then slowly, insidiously, brought herself to his side.

"Now, Ness . . ." he put in warily as he detected yet another game.

Her tone was gentle, cajoling, pleading; it was all these things, and it was totally arresting. "Bret, you don't mean to make Mary miss the height of the season simply because *I* am with child? You don't mean to make her wait, after she has been waiting so long already? Love, Mary is eighteen! Just think how uncomfortable I would be having Mary at Montlaine . . . when I know her heart is breaking for her first season! Bret, 'tis monstrous cruel. . . ."

His wife's hand had taken his own; she put it to her cheek and rubbed it on her smooth skin. "Bret . . . ?"

He was not immune to his wife's charms. Three years of marriage had only served to heighten his affection. He gently extracted his hand, but not without first pinching her cheek. "Naughty Ness . . . you play unfairly."

"And only think . . . Mary will be under my parents' wing. . . ."

"As you were?" His brow was up.

She wagged a finger at him. "Mary will give them no cause for alarm. Oh, Bret . . . ?"

He let go a sigh; clearly he was backed into a corner, and he was finding it most uncomfortable. A glance at Mary's hopeful countenance did him in. "Ness . . . *I* wanted to oversee Mary's first season," he returned pettishly.

"Well, and so you may. No one is asking you to

take your hand out of the pudding. You may leave instructions with my parents as to what you may or may not like." Again she was beside him, again her hand found his. "And after all, Bret, it is *you* who are insisting we return to Montlaine. I for one would rather remain in London and take on Mary's coming out!"

"Now, don't run me through, love." He was smiling down at her. "I want my child born at Montlaine. It is a particular wish . . ."

"Which I mean for you to have," she quickly broke in. "One would think that as I am being understanding . . . you would be the same?"

He gave up. He slipped his arm round her growing waistline and brought her closer still, forgetting for a moment his sister's watchful if silent presence. "So be it, then. Mary remains with your parents . . . and we are for Montlaine."

Lady Vanessa allowed him a smile, and her voice went soft, demure. "As my demon wishes. . . ."

Her husband was amused by her tactics. He had a strong urge to sweep her into his arms, but Mary deterred him by springing up to her feet and squeaking with delight, "Oh, Ness, Ness, you are the most complete hand!"

Her brother turned a frown on his wife. "You know what it is, Ness?" He shook his head. "She is picking up all manner of cant from that stripling brother of yours!"

"Oh, pooh!" returned his wife, taking Mary's hand and moving across to the hall door. "We have an afternoon's shopping to do, sweet demon,

and haven't a moment to lose. Come on, Mary."
With which they were gone.

Their bonnets and spencers dressing them
against the early spring chill, they stepped outside and would have then descended the white
stone steps to their waiting coach. However, a
jovial youth hailed them to attention.

"Ho, Ness ... Mary!" cried Lord Richard of
Grey as he hurriedly paid off the hackney driver
and made his way to them.

Instinctively Mary's hand flew up in greeting,
and then she stilled herself. This had not helped
in the past, this open affection she displayed toward him. She would have to stop it. She banished
the gleam and replaced it with a scarcely audible
greeting.

"Rick ... what is it? Mary and I were just
going out," said his sister.

"Must talk to you," he said on a breathless
note.

"Then come by later this afternoon."

"Can't. Must attend to the matter immediately, and you know, Ness, in this regard I think
you are the only person who can help me."

"Perhaps, Ness ... I should return to the house
and allow you to take a short walk with your
brother?" offered Mary quietly.

"Nonsense." Rick frowned. "We have no secrets,
Mary ... why should I exclude you?"

She thought of all the confidences she had heard
about all the different women he had fallen in

and out of love with these past three years and sighed. Sadly enough, it was true, he had few secrets from her. "Well then, perhaps, Rick, you would like to join us on our shopping expedition?" Mary tendered resignedly.

"Shopping? Dull sport, that. . . ." He tipped his gray top hat over his fair brows as he considered this. "I tell you what, though . . . I'll ride along with you as far as Bond Street. Mean to have a go at White's today anyway."

"Very well, then . . . come along, Rick," urged his sister, moving her charges toward the waiting coach.

Once settled within its confines, Lord Richard of Grey studied Lady Vanessa for a moment, and it goaded her into impatiently asking, "Well, what the deuce has you in such a tither, Rick?"

"It's Mrs. Clifford."

"What?" demanded his sister. "Never say you have seriously taken up with that woman?"

Her brother put up his chin. "Now, Ness . . . I must warn you that I will not hear a word of disparagement against her."

Mary turned away from this scene. It was one that sent prickling pins to torture. She attempted to block out the conversation from her mind.

"Oh, don't get your back up, Richard. I wasn't going to say anything about the woman. Why . . . how can I? I don't even really know her."

"No? Well, then . . ."

She cut him off at this. "However, when rumor had it that my brother was caught up in that

11

quarter, I assumed it was only a temporary thing."

He frowned at her. "Oh? Why would you assume that?"

"Well, dear . . . the widow is, I believe, older than you," she offered carefully.

He snapped his fingers and broke out into a grin. "Nina Clifford may be a widow, Ness, but Lord, she is only six and twenty!"

"And you are three and twenty," put in Mary quietly.

"What can that signify?" He turned on Mary, his mouth curved in disdain. "Three years? Tosh!"

"She is a widow. . . . Richard, her experience is bound to set her apart from you."

"You mean to suggest that she is more sophisticated?" His tone indicated that such a thought was ludicrous.

"I think," said Mary suddenly, "that we should hear what it is that Richard wants, before we start discussing such things."

Richard of Grey turned his bright-blue eyes on the dark-haired pretty. "Thank you, Mary. You are always to be counted on."

"Oh, very well," agreed his sister. "Just what do you want, Richard?"

He took a long gulp of air. "I should like to bring Mrs. Clifford around to our parents, Ness. . . ."

"Good Lord!" Vanessa was moved to ejaculate.

He bristled. "I don't see that my request is so outrageous as to send you into shock!"

"Don't you, my boy?" she returned hotly. "Well, then, it shows what little sense you have left!"

Mary put out her hand and stilled Richard. "Hold . . . both of you. Vanessa . . . surely there can be no objection to a small dinner party in which Mrs. Clifford is a guest?"

"No . . ." Ness returned warily. "But that is not what he asked . . . that is not what he wants. Is it, Richard?"

"Actually, no. I want a dinner for the select purpose of furthering my parents' acquaintance with Mrs. Clifford."

"That is not possible," returned Vanessa sharply.

"I don't see . . ."

"That is just it, you don't see!" she snapped. "If you think that Mama and Papa are going to approve of your courtship you are gravely mistaken!"

"I think," put in Mary, "your parents had a different type of woman in mind . . . for you."

"No doubt a prim and proper miss with no spirit!" he snapped. "Well, if you won't help me, Vanessa, it makes no odds, for I shall have the woman I want with or without their approval!"

The carriage had stopped in front of the steps that led to the world-famous men's club known as White's. He opened the door and would have left them on that parting note had not Mary held his arm.

"Richard . . . don't go in a huff. We will try to work something out."

He touched her gloved hand and gave her a half-smile. "Thank you, Mary. I can always rely on you to understand."

A moment later he was gone, and Vanessa was

staring hard at Mary. "Well?" she demanded at last.

"Well what, Nessie?" returned Mary, her impish smile lighting up her countenance.

"Stop that! I won't have it. Whatever do you mean, encouraging Richard in that direction?"

"I didn't." She shook her head. "*You* did."

"I?" Vanessa was clearly astounded by this accusation.

"Yes. You know what he is. No sooner has a denial been given to him than he will rush headlong to obtain that which has been denied. It is his way," said Mary on a knowing note.

"Is it indeed?" Vanessa was frowning. "Yes ..." she relented, "I suppose it is. But Mary ... what is to be done?"

"Allow him rein."

"He shall go hot and ready after *that woman*!"

"Will he? Perhaps. We shall see."

Vanessa started to say something, stopped herself and then said carefully, "Mary ... I thought ... at one time, you had a *tendre* for Richard."

"Did you think so? Perhaps I did."

"And now ... ?"

"And now, Vanessa, I am grown." Again that particular smile all her own, and Lady Vanessa eyed her thoughtfully. Her sister-in-law was bound to take the ton by storm. With that pert expression, who could resist her?

Chapter Two

The town house the Greys had long inhabited was situated in regal elegance on Berkeley Square. Its days had seen much, but the marriage of Vanessa had left the Greys sadly wanting. The servants had often sighed for some of the lighter exploits Vanessa had plunged them into. And then with Lord Richard setting up his own lodgings, they quite yearned for another youth to divert them. Their yearnings were certainly answered when Mary entered their scene.

Once again the house of Grey was thrown into a turmoil. There were a bevy of young cubs calling on Mary. The servants took an avid interest and chose their favorites among these. There was a constant hum and buzz about the house, for Mary was a small but lively bundle. She was discovered to be in every way a delightful imp of a girl, teasing one here, rallying another there, unreserved, brightly ingenuous and thoroughly enchanting.

Vanessa no longer was in London, as she had

departed with her husband for Montlaine, but the earl and his countess were soon seen to smile again, for Mary tickled at them until they were laughing. It was not, therefore, such a surprising thing that they should begin to hope for a match between Mary and their only son, Richard. Even the servants began to hope in that direction. However, Richard of Grey was not cooperating!

Rumor had it that he was dangling after the Clifford widow. It was, of course, absurd. Nina Clifford was worldly, he was not. Nina Clifford was an outrageous flirt, he was not. Nina Clifford was a selfish hedonist, putting her pleasure above all else, and he could not see this. But above all these things, Nina Clifford was *ton*. That fact made the situation sticky and very difficult to deal with.

Lady Grey paused from her letter-writing, and a sigh escaped her as she gazed out the window near her writing desk and watched a bird in flight in the small town garden. She wanted her son and Mary to make a match of it, but if Richard did not look in Mary's direction soon, it would be too late. This because although Mary had been out but two weeks, her list of suitors was growing. Mary had made a hit. She was hailed "a diamond of the first water," and it was something of a surprise, for she was not quite in style. The season called for tall blondes. Mary was a petite brunette. Lady Grey smiled to herself. It was Mary's eyes . . . they had a way of dancing, in tune to her mood, most engaging. If only Richard would notice. . . .

Mary looked up from her stitching and studied Lady Grey's lovely but thoughtful profile. She could see that something was troubling the countess, whom she had grown very fond of in the short time she had been staying with the Greys. What to do?

"Do you know, ma'am . . . that I have just hit upon a famous notion!"

"Have you, dear?" returned Lady Grey, coming out of her cogitations.

"Yes, just the thing for us, too. I read in the *Chronicle* this morning that there is an exhibition being given of Trevithick's latest steam engine. 'Tis being held at Crane's Wharf."

"Good gracious," cried her ladyship on a short laugh. "You are an atrocious child! There is no possibility, my dear, that I shall by any means of the imagination dislodge myself on such a doubtful excursion."

"Oh, but I am persuaded you would find it vastly entertaining, ma'am. Only fancy . . . it runs on the street . . . they mean to take on passengers. Shouldn't you like to go and have a look at the thing?"

"Have a look at what thing?" came an amiable voice from the sitting-room doorway.

Lady Grey looked up to find her son, fashionably (discounting the extreme points of his collar) attired in a dark-blue superfine sporting large brass buttons of questionable taste and pale-blue pantaloons. His fair hair was brushed in a semblance of disorderly curls, and his blue eyes seemed alert.

Mary as well as Lady Grey noted a certain undefinable something about his manner and were immediately set on guard.

"Mary here would have a look in at that dreadful machine everyone has been talking about. Would you credit it, Richard . . . the child means for me to accompany her," rallied Lady Grey with an end in mind.

Richard was willing enough to fall in with her aim, for he had one of his own. "No, Mary . . . really, you can't mean it. Ain't the thing for a female," he teased. "And Mama . . . what would she do there, for mark me, she won't set foot onto the Puffing Billy!"

She pulled a face at him. "Richard, you are being perfectly odious. Your mother has been cooped up all morning answering her mail. An outing would be just the thing."

"Not *that* outing!" he returned jovially and held up an admonishing finger. "Now, now, m'girl. Calm yourself. If you behave you will find that I might be disposed to escort you to the thing."

"Oh, Richard, would you?" She beamed. "I'll just run up and fetch my spencer."

"That's a good puss. . . ." He turned to his mother. "I'll ring round for Papa's phaeton, as I came in a hack. . . ."

This his mother was perfectly willing to allow, and a few moments later she was satisfied to see them off. Had she known the purpose in Richard's conciliation, she would have been less content indeed.

*　　*　　*

Mary allowed her gaze to wander from Richard's hands. He tooled his father's matched grays with a style that while not exacting enough to win him the tribute of being a notable whip, was certainly capable. From her place beside him on the perch phaeton she was able to survey the passing scenes, nod to acquaintances and feel very much the thing.

Richard stole a sideways glance. His young friend had in a matter of three years most certainly changed. For one thing, her mode of dress. It was nearly very shocking. Her white muslin gown was embellished with small red velvet hearts. Its cut was low enough to display the fact that her figure had blossomed; her spencer jacket tucked tightly at the waist did little to conceal at the bosom. This line of vision took him to her neck. Lovely. Adorned now with a wide white velvet ribbon from which a red ruby heart glistened alluringly. Further inquiry discovered rosy lips, fair cheeks . . . and then he was meeting her eyes. Dark, round and at the moment laughing.

"What . . . what is it you see?" He looked past her so that he too could find the jest.

"Look there . . . the Regent . . . oh, Richard, he has grown so fat he can scarcely manage to squeeze through the door of his carriage!"

Richard found this to be quite true, and they shared an easy chuckle together before he brought her attention around to himself. "Mary . . . there is something I particularly wanted to discuss with you. . . ."

"Aha! So that is why you are being so agreeable as to escort me on this expedition. I thought you had no interest in mechanical wonders!" accused Mary, not without some amusement to soften her words.

"Well, as to that . . . I should like to see Puffing Billy as much as you, so that is not quite entirely true."

"Give over then, Richard. What is it you want?" She believed in coming to the point without haggling.

"Since Vanessa chose to leave without putting in a word for me with regards to Mrs. Clifford . . . well, 'tis up to you, isn't it?" spilled from Richard of Grey's lips. Then, because he saw the astonishment in her eyes, "Well . . . what I mean is . . . my parents like you, Mary. If you were to add Nina's name to the list on one of the dinner parties m'mother is planning . . . well . . ."

Would he never see how she felt? Would he always take advantage of her? How could he ask her to do such a thing? She wanted to slap him. She wanted to shake him into a realization of her worth. She wanted to scream. Instead she gazed away from him and composed herself enough to turn and smile sweetly up at his expectant face.

"I shall certainly do whatever I can, Richard . . . though I won't promise anything will come of my endeavors."

He beamed brightly at her. "Mary, you are the best of good friends, and if I didn't have the reins to manage . . . I'd . . . I'd kiss you."

Quietly, so quietly he did not hear, she said softly, "Would you, Richard?"

"Eh? What's that, Mary?"

"Naught, Richard.... Mind, now ... you very nearly collided with that wagon!"

That very evening Mary was to make the Widow Clifford's acquaintance. Mary descended the stairs and found Richard awaiting her. He looked up and found her clothed in a filmy gown of pink sarsenet over pink satin. The material clung alluringly to her provocative lines, and he was struck once again with the realization that Mary was child no more. Her dark curls becomingly framed her piquant face, and her dark eyes glistened with the prospect of an evening at the Richmonds' fete.

"Mary! Why, Mary ... you look ravishing!" he expostulated, and then quickly before she could return in style, "Now ... hurry up, do, for the carriage is waiting."

"But what of your parents?" she returned in some surprise. "I thought they were to escort me ... and what the deuce are you doing here?"

Richard had some time ago set up his own establishment. It was becoming more and more an oddity to see him at the Greys' town house in Berkeley Square. He smiled.

"Mother sent a note around asking me to join the party. I thought I'd better, under the circumstances, you know.... Anyway ... going to the ball myself ..."

She understood all too clearly. "Ah, doing them up sweet, eh, Richard?"

"Well ... it wouldn't hurt. ..."

"But that doesn't explain where they have gone off to."

"Said as long as I was here to bring you along to the ball, thought they'd go off first and take up m'aunt with them. But never mind that now, Mary . . . my horses are standing!"

She allowed him to usher her quickly out of the house. He draped her velvet cloak about her shoulders as they made their way outdoors, and he remarked idly as he handed her up into his small but smart carriage, "You look wonderfully fetching with that feather curling around your ear, Mary."

She touched the pink fluff she had attached to her short dark curls, and a deep flush infiltrated her cheeks. "Why . . . thank you, Richard. My, all these compliments . . . whatever has got into you?"

He grinned broadly. "Well, m'girl . . . as you have been so obliging as to promise me your aid with regards to Mrs. Clifford . . ."

"Oh . . . I should have realized sooner, Richard, what you were about." The jest was in her voice, but all pleasure had departed.

The Richmonds' ball had scarcely begun, but the signs indicated great promise of its being a prodigious squeeze. All the ton flocked to this particular affair, for Lady Richmond was a hostess with considerable consequence among the beau monde.

Mary was deriving abundant enjoyment as she watched the passing parade of fashion. It was interesting to her to note that Brummell's mode of style reigned on in spite of his absence. Poor Brummell, he had fled London and his debts to live in obscurity in France. It was too bad, for often she had heard her brother speak admiringly of him.

Her hand was taken up for every dance, and even still she looked around the room for Richard, and then someone familiar caught her eyes. How she remembered those russet waves . . . so wildly did they frame his face, so provocative the dark-russet brows, so glittering those gray eyes. She could see them now; they were bright but held a note of boredom as he waltzed around the room with a pretty woman. She had a strong urge to call out his name. At last, the dance was ended, and putting propriety aside she nearly ran to catch him up.

"My lord?" she called on a gleeful note, too well pleased to see him again to put on sophisticated airs. He turned around and stared at her. She could see he did not know her, and she stamped her foot good-naturedly. "Oh, fie on you, Severn! Do you mean to say you don't remember me?"

He studied her a moment, a puzzled frown lighting his gray eyes. She was certainly as vibrant an imp as ever he had clapped eyes on. Bright and breathtaking to be sure, and while there was that about her that was oddly familiar, no, no he did not know her.

"Not remember you?" he answered at once and then gallantly bowed over her extended hand. "May I perish before ever I admit to such a thing."

She giggled. "Wretch. That is a rapper if ever I

23

heard one. But you mustn't feel stupid over this, as it has been an age since we have met, and while you have not changed one groat, I fancy I have."

He was intrigued. "You must give me a hint then, fair beauty . . . but first, let us find a space all our own." He took her hand and slipped it through his crooked arm and led her dexterously through a crowd to a quiet corner. He was Clinton, Lord Severn, and as such was forever being rushed after by matchmaking mamas. Now here was this chit charging at him with all her charms, and while he thought her efforts brazen, he was quite willing to play her game.

Mary was still a green girl. However, she realized soon enough that he was setting her up for a mild flirtation. It tickled her sense of humor. She would soon show him the error of his way, but for now was quite willing to play along . . . if only Richard would take notice.

"Very well, you asked for a hint. I shall describe our first encounter. . . ." There was a light in her eyes as she remembered this.

He took up her hand and would have placed it to his lips had she not withdrawn it and wagged a finger amicably but warningly. "Don't you want that hint . . . my lord?"

"By all means . . . our first encounter." Another light glistened in his eyes, and its heat was far more brazen than her behavior.

She was about to blurt out her name and the circumstances of their acquaintance before he forgot himself altogether, for she suddenly realized that his lordship (though he hid it well) was slightly in his cups; and then she saw Richard looking her way. She stopped herself and gave Lord Severn a bewitching smile.

"It was in the country . . . Cornwall . . . I shan't tell you where exactly . . . and it was six years ago."

He frowned. "Six years ago. . . . My dear, you couldn't have been more than a child."

"I was twelve . . . and rough-and-tumble as well. I was about to take my fence flying when you appeared out of nowhere . . . my horse stopped short of the fence . . . *but I didn't!*"

He took half a step backward and studied her. "Hold a moment . . . never say . . . Mary . . . Mary of Montlaine?"

She bowed her graceful head. "Aye, my lord." She then brightened. "Now do you remember?"

Six years ago. It had been an age. An age of disillusionments. He had gone to Montlaine with his friend, her brother, but he had not stayed above a sennight, and she had been a child. Here she was now a woman nearly grown, and he was approaching thirty. "How could I forget? What a brat of a girl you were. You ripped up at me before you had got to your feet!"

"And well you deserved it."

"Did I? Oh no, my girl, I did not. How did I know anyone was there?"

"Well, you shouldn't have come charging around a bend!" She was teasing, and her dark eyes were dancing until she saw Richard going across the room to greet the loveliest woman she had ever seen.

She broke off to ask, "My lord . . . who is that woman?"

He looked up to find the tall and elegant blonde enrobed in blue and silver taking up Richard of Grey's hand and moving onto the dance floor. He wondered fleetingly at Mary's interest but answered her query, "She is Nina Clifford, a notable widow . . . but Mary, why the interest?"

She forced herself to smile and look away from the pair on the dance floor. "Because I am as curious as ever. That was another thing that should have embedded me in your mind—I followed you all over Montlaine, forever plaguing you with my questions."

"Yes, and shoving discreditable frogs in my face and requesting to know their specific genre. You were perfectably detestable."

"Yes, and so I wonder at your attempt to dally with me, sir!" she returned on a laugh.

"I? I never did that!"

"Not then . . . but just a moment ago," she bantered.

He took up her hand, "I hear a waltz, and though my villainous behavior forbids me such a treat, I beg it all the same." He was already leading her out onto the floor.

She thought him very self-assured and would have withdrawn her hand and refused him the dance if only to set him down a peg, but Richard was on the floor and she had a need to be there as well. So it was that a moment later she found herself circling around in Lord Severn's arms and nearly touching Richard's elbow.

Lord Severn and Nina Clifford were well acquainted. Their eyes met and held a moment, and the lady smiled. He acknowledged it with the flicker of an eye. Richard did not notice this, but Mary did and frowned over it. However, a moment later the waltz ended and Richard, with Nina Clifford on his arm, was calling out her name.

"Mary . . . I say, Mary . . ."

Resigned to the inevitable, Mary turned to gaze upon her beautiful rival. Lord Severn, one russet brow arched with interest, lingered by her side.

"Mary . . . Mary . . ." said Richard on a breathless but happy note, "I should like to present Mrs. Nina Clifford to you." He turned a worshipful smile upon the blond goddess at his side. "Nina . . . Mary here has been a particular friend of mine. . . ."

"Yes, I am acquainted with your brother, Miss Montlaine." Nina smiled, but she was already looking past Mary and smiling coyly at Severn.

Mary presented his lordship, and Severn's eyes danced as he made Nina Clifford a bow. "Oh . . . Mrs. Clifford and I are very well acquainted."

Richard's blue eyes darkened over this remark, but Nina adroitly drew his attention away. "Richard . . . there is Lady Jersey. Do let us go and catch her before she runs off again, I have been wanting to speak with her."

Richard smiled, they were off, and Mary turned to find Lord Severn's gray eyes surveying her face. "The wind blows in that quarter, does it?"

"You are impertinent, my lord," she returned amicably enough.

He laughed. "So I am, but tell me, Mary . . . don't you approve?" His head nodded in the direction Richard and Nina had taken.

"I don't know what you mean," she returned carefully.

"Don't you? I rather thought you might . . . young Grey did refer to you as a particular friend."

"And as his particular friend, I don't discuss his affairs with strangers," she returned.

"Oho! So then now I am a stranger!" he bantered.

She blushed. "Well, no . . . no, you are not . . . but you know perfectly well what I mean."

"So I do." He did not pursue the matter, and it was at this moment that her hand was solicited for a country dance.

Mary went through a whirlwind of dances, and when next she looked for Lord Severn he was gone. She was sorry for it. She was concerned lest he had taken affront at her last remark, but there was nothing she could do but hope to set things right and tight at their next encounter.

It was some moments later that Richard took up her hand and informed her that Mrs. Clifford had departed the ball with a headache and that his parents had also left. It was up to him to see her home. She remarked rather unwisely that she was surprised he had not escorted Mrs. Clifford home.

"Mary! What a green puss you are. How would that have looked? All the tattlemongers would have started in on me, and then I'd be pickled. No, don't want to get m'parents' backs up."

Their ride home together found them unusually

silent, until Richard finally dropped his finger which had been bent over his pursed lips and ventured a sigh.

"You know, Mary . . . Severn, he ain't the sort I like to see you dangling after."

"Odious noddy! Dangling after indeed. I did no such thing."

"Well, that don't signify. What does is that he ain't the sort of company for you to keep."

She should have been pleased that he noticed what she did, with whom she had spent her time. Until that moment she hadn't been aware that he had given a fig about how she spent the evening. His remark, however, had provoked her, and she put up her chin.

"Careful, Richard. Severn is a friend of my brother's."

"Now don't pucker up at me, Mary. What I am trying to say is . . . well, Severn is a regular out-'n'-outer . . . a high flyer . . . a nonesuch . . . a whipster, but Mary . . . you'd be nothing but a gapeseed if you thought him anything but a . . . a . . ."

"A rake," she supplied. "Yes, I know . . . so was my brother."

"But your brother ain't now . . . Vanessa sees to that. Severn still is!"

"And I suppose sweet Mary is too untutored in such things to know how to go on?" she snapped.

"Well, as to that . . . look, Mary, I am not saying that Severn would play fast and loose with you. He generally steers clear of marriageable maids. His tastes run to the light skirts . . . you are quality. But he did pay you particular attention tonight, and I wanted you to realize that . . ."

"I realized that he found me excessively attractive and that I am also the sister of one of his close friends," she answered fulminatingly.

They both lapsed once again into silence until Richard cleared his throat. "What . . . what did you think of her?"

"Of whom?" she answered sweetly.

He frowned. "Why, of Mrs. Clifford, of course."

"Oh . . . yes, she was very lovely, Richard. A bit tall for you, I thought . . . but very lovely."

"Tall. But I am taller than Nina."

"Are you? I must be mistaken, then."

He frowned over this. "Must have been her curls . . . she piled 'em on high . . . but Lordy, Mary, her shoulder scarcely makes mine."

"It doesn't matter, Richard, truly." She paused. "She is . . . very beautiful."

"Yes, and witty, too, Mary. She is . . . wonderful."

Mary digested this and then said cautiously, "She . . . she seems to be on close terms with Severn."

"Did you think so?"

"Yes, but never mind. . . . I suppose it's because they have a deal in common . . . being so close in age to one another." She bit her lip as soon as this was out. She hadn't meant to be so waspish, but it was more than mind and heart could bear to hear him go on about a woman who was so ill suited to him.

He stared coldly at her. "That remark was beneath you, Mary."

She reached out and touched his white-gloved hand. "It was excessively ill bred of me, Richard. I . . . beg your pardon."

He grinned suddenly and lifted her own gloved hand to his lips and dropped a light kiss upon her wrist. It should have thrilled her; it only made her want to cry.

"Mary . . . oh, Mary, you could never be ill bred. Now, when do you mean to work Mrs. Clifford's name onto Mama's guest list?"

Mary struggled with herself before answering, "Soon, Richard, soon."

Chapter Three

It was the morning after the Richmonds' ball and Mary could not sleep. Thoughts varied, conflicting and emotional tugged at her heart. She was considered to be the season's incomparable. She was sought after, flattered, entertained, and she was miserable. This arose from two demoralizing realizations. One, she realized that her fortune as much as (if not more than) anything had added to her consequence and set her as a "catch." The other, she had not the wiles to win Richard's heart. Did she want his heart? Yes. For three years, from the first moment of seeing him at Penrod Tower, she had been thoroughly infatuated with him. There was a time when she thought he might return her affection, yet here she was watching him make a cake of himself over a woman who cared not a jot for him!

She slipped into her olive-green riding habit and fastened the black frogging over the ivory silk blouse. A matching top hat of olive green was propped at an angle over her short dark curls. She appraised herself. She was certainly no Nina Clifford. That woman had a certain sensuality . . . a certain something . . . experience. That was it, of course. Nina Clifford wanted Richard of Grey, and she meant to have him. How then to protect Richard from such a fate?

She pulled on her kid gloves and left her room. There was no one about but the parlor maid, who immediately rang for Tootles, the butler. Tootles, an elderly retainer with a great deal of countenance and composure, might have thought it odd for Miss Montlaine to wish to go riding at such an unfashionable hour, but there was nothing in his manner to indicate this as he sent a footman around to fetch her horse and a groom to attend her ride.

Some moments later Mary was enjoying a heady pace through Hyde Park. There was no cause for concern, as few people of notable consequence were about to observe her swiftly styled canter. It was a good feeling, tame compared to the wilds of Cornwall, but good all the same. She took in rein and collected her mare's canter into a rocking gait that was as comfortable as though she were floating through the air. Finally she slowed her mare to a jog and took in the early-morning view. The park's rolling lawns were richly green. The daffodils were just beginning to spurt forth in yellow glory, and the hour held a mist that gave it all a storylike aura. She sighed to think that in a few hours' time the sereneness of the park would be blasted away with the teeming, buzzing flow of fashionables on the strut.

Her groom called her attention to a passing vendor selling sweet rolls, but she turned this down. It was time to return home and attend Lady Grey. It was time to procure an invitation for Mrs. Clifford for the dinner party Lady Grey was throwing the following week. As she turned her mare homeward, a familiar form came into view. He was jogging his horse toward her, and excitement filled her breast as his features became more distinct. Yellow waves beneath a sporting top hat. A lanky build squeezed into a riding coat of dark-blue superfine. Legs too thin for the buff-colored breeches and Hessians exquisitely polished. As she drew her horse up she could see his blue eyes fill with astonishment. The face resembled those of the house of Grey, for, indeed, he was a close cousin. Lord Southvale put up his hand.

"Mary! By Jove . . . it is, isn't it?"

"Well, of course it is, who else would accost you in this manner, noddy?" said Mary, extending her hand to him and throwing him a warm kiss.

Randall, Lord Southvale, had not seen her since Christmas last. Less than a year had passed, and yet an undefinable air of difference lay between the Mary of then and the Mary of now. She was a woman. Alluring, provocatively shaped, and no longer sporting schoolclothes. Her hair . . . it was fashioned differently . . . there was a touch of blacking to her lashes . . . a hint of ingenuous coquettishness about the mouth.

"But . . . Mary . . . you . . . you look . . . different," said he, taking in a gulp of air.

She laughed. "Well, I have been brought out, you see."

"Zounds, girl, so you have. Missed it . . . had to attend to matters at my estate."

Lord Southvale had recently come into his title and inheritance, as his father had passed away the year before. It had wrought a change in him. In age, tastes and disposition he had very nearly matched his cousin, Richard. They had happily grown to manhood much in each other's way and were the best of friends. However, forced responsibilities had torn Randall away from his rackety style.

"Yes, and that is not all you have missed, Randall. I am so glad you are back, for there is something very particular I wish to discuss with you."

"Is there?" He looked worried. Mary had in the past drawn Richard and him into larks, some of which had had serious consequences. He was not sure he wanted to be involved in a scrape of her making at this time. "Well . . . glad to help, Mary . . . but on m'way to Richard's lodgings now . . . perhaps later."

"No, and it is about Richard that we must speak."

"Is it?" He was surprised and interested. "Why?"

She indicated with her eyes that her groom was within hearing distance, and Randall wondered flittingly when it was that she had begun to worry over the proprieties; she never had done so before.

"Randy . . . let us return home, where we may be comfortable over a pot of coffee, and then I shall tell you what I want you to do."

"But Mary . . ."

Again she used her eyes, this time quite differently, and the effect was remarkable. "Do you mean to play off an excuse to *me?*"

Randall of Southvale was lost to that look, to that inquiry. He discovered that his initial pursuit was naught next to her desire. He was in no measure proof against her wiles. She entreated with eyes that were both dark and tantalizing. All his plans for that morning's enjoyment were shot to pieces.

"Cry off indeed!" he returned gallantly.

She laughed and clicked her tongue. Her horse moved easily into a trot, and both riders were off in a spirited mood with Mary's groom trailing behind. Some twenty minutes later saw them with their heads together in the Greys' drawing room. Its apple-green decor made an outstanding contrast for Mary's loveliness, and every minute found Randall more conscious of this fact.

Finally she thought it time to plunge in. "It's Mrs. Clifford, Randy!"

"Is it? Never said I was needle-witted, but dash it, girl, what are you talking about?"

"Nina Clifford and . . . and . . . Richard," she wailed softly.

"Eh? No! Upon my word . . . never say Rick is

37

still dangling after her?" Randy was moved to expostulate dubiously.

"It is far more serious than that. Randy . . . I . . . I . . . oh, Randy . . ." she cried tragically. "I think he means to marry the woman!"

"Dashed if I believe that!" returned Randy acidly. "What has put such an absurd notion into your head?"

"He has," answered Mary simply.

"Eh? He has?" returned Randy on a stunned note. He put his hand to his chin to think this through and shook his head doubtfully over the information. "Well, if he thinks Nina Clifford will have him, he has maggots in his head!"

This so startled Mary that she stood up in defense of him. "Why shouldn't she have him?"

"Nina Clifford and Rick? It's laughable."

"You are very much mistaken," returned Mary, chin well up. "She means to wed him, and soon!"

"He is daft if he has told you that!"

"He hasn't told me that . . . I witnessed it with my own eyes. Randy, believe me . . . Richard's suit is not disagreeable to her."

"But . . . but . . . Nina Clifford . . . she is quite all the crack! I mean, if she wanted a duke it would be within her power to have one."

"Dukes," returned Mary dryly, "are hard to come by, while Richard is heir apparent to an earldom and vast estates!"

This struck Randy hard. He stared at Mary a moment and then shook his head again. "Still . . . Richard's a boy . . . next to her, I mean. . . ."

"Yes, precisely so, Randy. While she is, she is . . ."

"Careful, Mary," he interrupted gravely. "Nina Clifford is ton. She is accepted by Ladies Sefton and Jersey . . . she is one of London's leading hostesses . . . she comes of good stock . . . she is . . ."

"Yes, I know, she is a lady . . . but Randall, she has the soul of a courtesan!" snapped Mary, forgetting herself a moment.

"So she does . . . but it is not the thing for you to be knowing or talking about," he reproved.

"You are forgetting that Montlaine is my brother. There are a great many things I have learned about through him that most gently nurtured maids don't have the opportunity to learn," said Mary, summarily putting an end to whatever scold he might have had in mind.

"Eh . . . that may be true . . . but . . ."

"But we must do something, Randall."

"Do something?" returned Randall of Southvale on an uneasy note. Care for his cousin he did. Had he in fact been called upon for a dangerous deed on Richard's behalf, he would have dived in wholeheartedly, but intrude upon his cousin's private affairs he would not. "I don't think we can," he said gravely.

"Don't be so stuffy, Randy. You don't mean to tell me that we shall stand by and allow that woman . . . that woman to ensnare Richard? Why, she would play him false and break his heart in the end. Randy, he is in earnest . . . and she . . . she means only to have his money and marry into the house of Grey!"

He gave this his thoughtful consideration and sighed. "The thing is, Mary, that when I left

Rick, he was taken with Nina Clifford, but *not* to that extent.... I mean, it wouldn't be the first time Rick has made a cake of himself over a pretty woman ... fact is, we both have, more times than I care to count, and we are both still enjoying the single state!"

She was about to answer him in strong accents when Lady Grey entered the room. Her ladyship wore a morning dress of soft brown velvet. Its collar was made of a wide lacy material. This trim was carried to the cuffs of the sleeves as well, and she made an elegant figure. Her cool blue eyes took in the scene thoughtfully before she put out her hands to her nephew, who rose and came forward in warm greeting. "Randall, dear, how very good to have you with us once again. How does your mother go on at Southvale? I had quite expected that she would be bored to pieces long before this and insisting on returning to London."

He dropped a light kiss upon his aunt's cheek and grinned. "As to that, Mama has involved herself with the lives of one of our tenants and does not mean to leave Southvale until she has sorted their mess out right and tight!"

"Bother, I am pining for her company." Lady Grey sighed. "But that is Deborah all over...." She turned to Mary. "Good morning, dear. Did you enjoy your early ride in the park?"

"Yes." She looked at Lady Grey a moment, then smiled. "That's it ... I knew there was something different. You have done your hair differently. It looks lovely."

Lady Grey patted the short finely white-tinged blond waves. "Why, thank you, Mary. And now will you amuse me by telling me what had your heads together when I first walked in?"

Guiltily lad and lass exchanged glances before Mary hastily took the conversation by the horns. "Oh, I have just been telling Randall what a hit I have become and how infamous it was of him to go away just as I was being brought out."

"Ah, I see," said Lady Grey, perfectly well aware that her young protégée was shamming it. She moved to the coffee table and poured out three cups, all the while making idle chatter. She handed a cup to Mary and another to Randall before taking up her own.

Mary hesitated and then in her fashion dove right in, shocking Randall into nearly choking over his first sip of the hot brew.

"I . . . I noticed the invitations for that dinner you and Lord Grey are giving next week don't include Nina Clifford . . . ?" It was piece of impertinence on her part. She knew it and waited anxiously to see if her ladyship would give her a set-down.

Lady Grey's brow went up warningly. "Nooo . . . her name never entered my mind." And then, as an afterthought, "Why, Mary, should you imagine that Mrs. Clifford would be on my list? I think I mentioned that although the party numbers some forty people, they are our own select group . . . family and close friends only."

"Richard mentioned the affair to me . . . you see. . . ."

"No, I don't see."

"Richard also mentioned that he . . . he would be pleased to find Mrs. Clifford had been invited."

"Mary . . . I say . . . only think . . ." put in Randy on a note of concern, for he could see that her ladyship was not pleased.

"No, Randall . . . it must be said," retorted Mary daringly. "You see, ma'am . . . as it is a particular wish of Richard's . . . I thought it might be prudent to . . . favor him in this regard. I have thought a great deal about it. You must realize that no one wishes Nina Clifford at Jericho more than I, but she is not someone who will vanish simply because I wish it." Mary sighed. "She is a problem that must be faced . . . and perhaps we are wrong about her . . . about the match."

Lady Grey had been frowning but mulling Mary's words over carefully. The chit had good sense. She looked up at this last remark, however. "No, we are not wrong about Nina Clifford. She is not what I want for my son. However, you may be right. He should observe how she goes on among his family . . . his closest friends. It will be interesting to see if her behavior among us might instill a change of feeling in him. . . . Yes, Mary, an invitation shall go out to Nina Clifford!"

Randall clucked his tongue. "As for me, I think it is all a hum. I mean . . . Rick is no slow top . . . he knows what Nina Clifford is . . . at least I thought he knew. . . ." He moved to pick up his top hat and gloves. "I think I'll go pay my cousin a visit."

Mary reached out her hand and stayed him a moment, and he was struck once more by her beauty. Could it be that he had never seen her before? In these three last years had he never really looked? An odd thrill rushed through him as he felt her fingers on his hand.

"Do be tactful, Randy . . . don't allow him to see what you are after or that any of us disapproves."

He patted her fingers. "Don't fret, Mary, you can trust me." With that he nodded to his aunt and was gone.

"Now," said Lady Grey, turning her attention to Mary, "I will write out that invitation, and you will rush upstairs and change your riding clothes." She smiled at Mary's surprise. "We have an appointment at Madame Renée's. . . ."

It did not take long for Randall to fetch his horse from the Greys' stable and make his way to his cousin's lodgings. It took an imperious air to thrust his hat and gloves into Richard's butler's austere embrace and sweep past him to Richard's private rooms. There he found his cousin still in his nightclothes but on the verge of rising. "Aha, so there you are, you frippery fellow!" exclaimed Randall merrily enough.

Richard grinned. "Egad! What do you mean barging in on me at this hour?"

"There is an exhibition being held in Gentleman Jackson's salon. Thought you would want to accompany me. Come on, up with you, monsieur slug!"

"Ho . . . never say you came all the way back

from Southvale just for the pugilism exhibition!"

"That and a few other interests of mine," said Randall slowly, grinning.

"Yes, like that yella-haired opera singer, I'd wager." He shook his head amicably, "Well, you are out there ... I think Severn has a pretty tight grip in that direction."

"Has he?" Randy sighed for his loss. "Thought as much would happen as soon as I left London. No matter. Now, up with you."

Richard of Grey got to his feet, stretched wide, smiled, then quickly, playfully lunged his fist at his cousin's belly. Randy sidestepped, but not in time, and groaned dramatically as he bent over the blow. "Shabby trickster!" With which both lads came to gleeful fisticuffs. The bout left them laughing and ready for an outing in each other's company.

Randy sighed as he watched his cousin slip into his fashionable garments, and he was fraught with doubt. Finally, he forced himself to say, "So tell me ... how is the lovely Mrs. Clifford?"

"As lovely as ever," returned Richard.

"Thought as much ... but do you see her ... often?"

"As often as I may," answered Richard.

"And ... ?"

"And what, Randall?" There was a warning there.

"Well ... dash it, Rick ... she ain't an opera singer, is she?"

"I should say not. Will you tell me what you are getting at?"

"Want to know how you feel about her . . . want to know . . . what you intend."

Richard ran his hand through his fair hair. "Feel? I'm . . . in the throes of agony, Randy . . . I want to possess her. I am sick with jealousy when another man makes her laugh. I . . . damn . . . I don't know how I feel."

Randall was not encouraged by this. However, he thought it prudent to allow the subject to cease at this point. Therefore he related in an amusing style one of his mother's latest escapades, and Nina Clifford was for a time put aside.

She was, however, still uppermost in Mary's thoughts. Our maid stood idly as she watched Lady Grey try on a succession of hats. Finally she released a sigh and ventured casually, "I could go across the street and pick up those books I wanted from the circulating library."

"What, love? Oh . . . yes, the books. What a very excellent thought. Go on, dear, I shall wait for you here."

Mary smiled to herself, for she could see her ladyship was having a marvelous time trying on hat after hat. She dipped and adjusted her own lovely pink confection atop her dark curls, straightened the cut of her pink spencer, and sallied forth.

It was well past noon, and the street was teaming with afternoon traffic. Yellow wheels. They caught her eye. Her attention was taken up by as exquisite a piece of workmanship as ever she had seen. She didn't think even her own brother's phaeton as neatly styled as the high-perch equipage coming around the bend. It happened just at that moment. So quickly she didn't realize what she was doing. So quickly that only instinct moved her, reflex action came into play.

A toddler no older than three caught sight of something in the road and decided he must have it. He escaped his governess's charge and darted out. The driver of the perch phaeton saw him and swerved, but even so he was so close, too close . . . and then Mary was there, scooping up the child and pitching him out of harm's way!

Mary tripped over the curbing, but the little fellow landed upright and exhibited his fright at that point in resonant detail. This, however, was scarcely heard over his governess's caterwauling and the commotion of the growing crowd.

Mary started to get up, felt a sharp pain just beneath one knee, winced and then suddenly felt herself hoisted up by strong firm hands. She was conscious of extreme strength, an air of self-assurance, and then she heard her name.

"Mary!" exclaimed Lord Severn, the driver of the nefarious vehicle at the heart of all this frenzy. "Are you hurt?"

She looked up and found his gray eyes, stern, disapproving. She felt her pride pinched. With a wry smile she could see that her gown was torn in several places, her spencer dirtied, her hat felt askew and her knee out of joint, yet here he was looking a stricture at her. "No, my lord, how should I be?" And then more waspishly, "What the deuce do you mean driving at such a mad pace on such a busy street?"

46

He was maneuvering her away from the crowd, more quickly now as the slew at her back seemed to pick up on this question. She found herself ushered toward his phaeton, which was held at a standstill by his small and wide-eyed tiger. "Come on, Mary, this is no place for you."

"But ... but ... my lord ..." she objected, attempting to withdraw herself out of his firm grasp. "Her ladyship ... Lady Grey ... awaits my return in the milliner's shop. ..."

He nodded at his young groom. "My lad will convey the message to her that I have seen you safely home. You will explain all to her later, and she will fully understand and agree with my decision to spirit you away from this rabble!" With this he lifted her autocratically onto the high seat above, went around, jumped nimbly into place on the seat beside her, took up the reins and tooled his vehicle forward and neatly away from the chagrined crowd.

Mary brushed off some of her dirt and turned to look ruefully up at him. "I never appreciated how masterful you are, my lord!"

"And I never realized how stupid you could be, Mary!" he snapped.

She was understandably incensed at this. She had just accomplished a daring feat and one that spared him the guilt of injuring a child. Now while she might have expected gratitude, it would have embarrassed her to receive it. This, however, was an insufferable attitude. She nearly spluttered, so intense was her agitation. "Stupid?

47

I . . . stupid? How dare you? There was a babe . . . he ran directly in your path . . ."

"He had already halted his progress, and *I* executed a very neat swerve out of his path!" returned his lordship angrily. "Your interference attracted an unnecessary mob and could have caused you some injury!"

"Well, it did not!" Mary's dark eyes were burning with angry sparks, and he noted that even in her disheveled state she was quite a taking thing when angry.

Ridiculously this fleeting thought softened his mood. At that moment they had pulled up before the Greys' town house and a footman came to hold the horse's heads. Lord Severn flipped a coin into the lackey's gloved hand and requested him to care for the horses while he escorted Miss Montlaine within doors.

"There is no need for you to accompany me." Mary had her chin well into the air, but as she started to descend she came down hard on the injured leg and was all too aware of a shooting pain that journeyed through her calf and ended by throbbing at her kneecap. She could not help but cry out, and the sound brought Lord Severn to her side immediately. His arm went around her, for he could see from her paled countenance that she was in need of physical support. This he amply provided as he ushered her past Tootles, who held the front door opened wide for their entrance.

Tootles immediately saw that the situation

called for action, and hastily he sped ahead to open wide the library door.

Lord Severn brought Mary, who limped only slightly, to the room and threw over his shoulder, "Have some hot tea brought in . . . and a hot bath prepared for Miss Montlaine."

"Very good, sir." Tootles had no idea who the gentleman might be; however, he recognized leadership and responded to it without question. If he was curious, he had the training to hide it well.

Once inside the spacious and elegantly styled bookroom, he set Mary down on the fashionably upholstered yellow sofa and peremptorily removed her hat and began undoing her top spencer buttons.

"What are you doing?" she asked sharply, simultaneously slapping away his hands.

He chuckled amicably. "Making you comfortable, little spitfire, so calm yourself in the sure knowledge that I shall not ravish you in Lady Grey's home."

She smiled over this, and then her eyes twinkled, though her voice took on a serious vein. "Of course . . . what am I thinking of? That would be the height of impropriety, I suppose."

He responded to this by flicking her pert nose. "Quite." A frown formed his brows and he said on a note of doubt, "Mary, would you let me raise your skirt . . . just high enough to have a look at that knee of yours?"

"Careful now, my lord . . . I do believe you are

making me an improper proposition." She was bantering.

"I take it, then, that you won't let me have a go at that leg of yours?" He was grinning.

"How percipient of you." She relented and said more amicably, "At any rate, it is the veriest bruise and will be better after the bath you have so kindly ordered put to for me."

He cocked his head, wondering whether she was thanking him in her odd way or poking fun at his earlier imperiousness. However, it was just then that the tea tray was brought in and laid before him on the satinwood table. He had been sitting on the sofa beside Mary. He turned to the teapot and busied himself preparing her a cup. He put it into her hands,

"Drink, my girl!"

"Yes, sir!" she answered sharply and did not make any attempt to do so.

He smiled. "Please, Mary . . . it will do you good."

She eyed him a moment, sipped and then said lightly, "You may go now, my lord. Really, you have quite outdone whatever duty you may have felt was due me."

"Due you? What was due you was a sound thrashing!" He put up his hand at her rising anger. "Careful, now . . . here is Lady Grey."

The countess entered the room and stepped forward, allowing his lordship, who had risen and gone to her, to take up her outstretched hands. "My lord Severn . . . what is all this . . . your boy said something about a near accident.

Mary . . . ?" She was moving to where Mary had twisted around on the sofa to face her. "Mary, are you all right?"

"I believe Miss Montlaine has suffered something of an injury. However, she would not allow me to attend her," put in his lordship.

Mary pulled a face at him and then turned a smile upon Lady Grey's concerned countenance. "Please, ma'am . . . it is nothing. I have tried to explain that to Lord Severn."

A lackey appeared with the announcement that Miss Montlaine's bath was ready and awaiting her pleasure. She took this as her means of escape, rose to her feet, stifled the pain and stiffly took her leave of them.

Lady Grey turned an inquiring eye upon his lordship. "Now, my friend, would you mind explaining . . . and in detail?"

He put a hand through his russet hair and sighed. "Not at all, my lady. . . ." With which he set her worry aside.

Chapter Four

Lord Severn was a friend of Mary's brother's. More than this she knew too that he traveled in the first circles, that he was a nonesuch of some repute and that he was considered a rakehell. She did not realize, however, how very much influence he exerted over society's fribbles until she encountered him three nights after their fracas over the toddler.

Mary was a decided hit with the beau monde. She was enchantingly lovely. She was a lively ingenue. She was a Montlaine, and it was known that she was a modest heiress. She did not want for suitors—how could she? However, it was on this particular evening that she learned the difference between making a mildly successful debut and becoming "all the crack."

Lord Severn, looking his best in the black dress clothes Brummell had brought into fashion, was seen to take the trouble of seeking Mary of Montlaine out, and swiftly whispers began. He was, after all, in spite of his cavalier address quite a marriage prize.

"Mary . . . how are you?" he said softly, turning her attention away from the young cub she had been conversing with and bringing her dark eyes to his face.

There he stood, looming above her, his gray eyes bright, his rugged countenance captivating, his layered waves of russet-gold hair framing his handsome face, and all she could do was stiffen and reply lightly that she was well. She turned once again to the hopeful cub.

His lordship was not to be put off. He was but scarcely acquainted with the youth; however, he directed a meaningful glare his way.

"Miss Montlaine would, I am sure, enjoy a glass of lemonade. . . ."

The lad was not dense. He saw Miss Montlaine begin to object, but he also knew that this was a sign that Lord Severn wanted private conversation with her. He was not in a position to incur this notable's displeasure. He bowed himself away, saying that he would return directly with the treat.

Mary put up her chin. "That was neatly contrived, my lord."

"Yes, I thought so."

"But then . . . *he* was no match for you."

"And, sweet Mary . . . *you are?*" He already had her hand and was leading her onto the dance floor in time to the waltz that was struck up.

She protested feebly, for she had no wish to make a scene and she noticed that people were looking their way. Fleetingly she wondered at it. He was twirling her around the floor, but she had put on a face. She would show him that he could not play off his tricks with her!

He looked at her set countenance, threw back his head and released a short laugh. "Mary . . . whatever you do, don't scowl. People will imagine the oddest things."

"I am still very angry with you," she retorted candidly. "You did not behave very handsomely the other day."

"Ah, I am in your black books, then? What can I do to retrieve myself?"

She looked at him and found his eyes. A mistake, she told herself at once. He had *such* eyes. "Perhaps you can't, my lord."

"Now didn't someone very important . . . very well respected . . . say something about forgiving being divine?"

"Alexander Pope. Do you then admit that you erred?"

"No."

"Then why should I forgive?"

"Because, my sweet Mary . . . you *are* divine." it was said with just such a look, just such a tone. It was calculated to level her to a blush.

It missed its mark. Mary was looking across at Richard waltzing with Nina Clifford. He followed her gaze and frowned. Lord Severn felt a touch of pique. Here he was flirting with this chit. Why? Partly because she was the sister of a close friend and he sincerely wanted to ensure her season, and partly because he found her intriguing enough to engage her in a mild flirtation. But did she appreciate what he was doing for her? No. She seemed in fact oblivious to the honor being bestowed upon her. Again he watched her as her eyes followed Richard and Nina Clifford, and he wondered again if the wind flowed in that direction.

"They make an attractive couple."

"What? Who?" she answered, startled.

"Young Grey and Mrs. Clifford."

She pulled a grimace. "You can't mean it!"

"Well, perhaps he is a bit young for her."

"You mean, she is a bit old for him!" returned Mary, staunchly loyal.

He laughed. "It appears nevertheless that she means to have him. Surprising, but there it is."

"I don't find it surprising, and if there is anything *I* can do about it, I shall!"

"Oh? Why?"

"Because . . . because . . . never mind. I really shouldn't be talking in this fashion with you."

"Why not? Are we not friends?" He was amused by her confusion.

"I don't know," she answered. "Are we?"

"Yes, Mary. Yes, we most certainly are."

The waltz was at an end, but he stood for another ten minutes adroitly engaging her in harmless banter. This fact was noted by many of the assembled company, and it was whispered that Mary of Montlaine had caught Severn's fancy. Her season was ensured. She went from the numbering belles to number one on the board. If Severn was taken with her, Severn, the connoisseur of incomparables, she must be something special indeed.

It was therefore not surprising that her list of suitors doubled and that Lady Grey's house was the next morning inundated with morning callers. Lady Grey sighed to her amused spouse. "Severn has quite brought Mary into the height of fashion. She will have any number of offers very soon now."

"How very obliging of Severn. Why do you seem put out?" inquired the earl, one fair brow raised quizzically. He knew all too well why his lady was unhappy, but it tickled him to tease her.

"You know very well what my hopes are in that regard." She hesitated, a frown drawing her delicate brows severely. "I rather thought, in fact, that . . . *we* were in accord in this . . . ?"

He patted her shoulder reassuringly. "My dearest love, we most certainly are in accord in our wishes. However, wanting something and having it are two very different things. We are virtually helpless in this situation. We can do naught presently but watch, and it is, my dear, all very, very amusing."

Lady Grey was not in agreement with this mode of thought and thus left her husband to his papers and took the stairs in something of a huff. How could he be so cool when his son was flaunting an affection for a woman who was totally unsuitable? This was callous behavior indeed! Then too, how *her* son could pass by Mary without the slightest interest was beyond everything unhappy, especially when Mary was quite

57

the most sought-after maid this season. And if all this was not enough to shatter one's nerves, there was Severn paying particular attention to Mary. What had he to do with Mary? He was a rogue, a scamp of a flirt, but he rarely dallied with young flowers. She would have to see to it that Mary did not mistake the man's outrageous flirting for anything but what it was.

It was in this frame of mind that Lady Grey entered her drawing room to find Mary enjoying an animated conversation with an extraordinary quantity of young blades. It was, of course, very gratifying to have first launched a daughter who had been a triumphant success and now to discover too that her protégée would find her own season no less victorious. While she took pride in this circumstance, a sigh escaped her all the same, for a quick glance around the room told her that while Randall of Southvale numbered among Mary's crew, her son did not!

It was an early hour for Lord Severn to be up and about. It was, in fact, an even earlier hour for him to be on his way to Francine White's establishment in Mayfair, but he was restless, fidgety, without appetite for food or sport and unable to ascertain the cause for his mood. It occurred to him that the lady might while away an hour or two, and this was his mood when he pulled up his team outside her house.

Nimbly Severn jumped out of his smart-looking phaeton, handed the reins to his young tiger, smiled and arched a brow.

"Mind now, lad, I'll have your skin if you so much as put one scratch to my yellow wheels!"

The boy grinned broadly, for he knew full well that his employer trusted him with both the high-stepping horses before him and the well-built carriage beneath him. It was an honor, and he beamed proudly as he watched Severn turn and walk to the narrow, three-story brick building that housed Severn's latest mistress.

His lordship was shown into the dark hallway by a nervous and rather lanky young maid who couldn't meet his eyes when she advised him that her mistress was still abovestairs.

Severn's eyes twinkled with mild amusement, but he returned an answer that he knew the way well enough and proceeded up the stairs, leaving the blushing girl at his back.

Francine White was an opera singer with a great deal of beauty and very little talent. She had worked hard to achieve her success, and there was a touch of bitterness in her for the role fate had assigned her. She sat now at her vanity examining her features with a sense of consternation. She was nearly five and twenty. Five and twenty and still only some man's mistress. However, he was not just any man! This was Severn. He was a nobleman, he was wealthy, young, virile and eligible as well.

She wanted to be his wife. Preposterous was what her inner sense told her. Impossible. She was a courtesan, and her class was beneath, so far beneath, his own. It wasn't fair. Hadn't the Gunning sisters achieved spectacular marriages, and there wasn't anything to choose between herself and them, was there? Was it wrong to want to have such a marriage? No, and no again. Therefore she would have to use whatever tools were at her command to achieve her aspirations.

Severn! A high star indeed, and far more difficult to entrap than some of the men and boys who had begged for her favors, but Severn was certainly worth the extra effort. She did not love him, doubted that she would ever love any man of his sort, for she knew them for what they were, all they could ever be. Severn . . . how to win his heart, how to gain his name?

He opened the door and found her sitting in red lace facing her mirror, and there was an expression on her face that instantly repelled him. He stood a moment and then called her name softly, bringing her to face him.

"Francine . . . ?"

She turned, and her long bright-gold ringlets swayed with the movement. Whatever was he doing here at this hour? Was it an indication that he cared far more than he showed?

"Darling. What a wonderful surprise," she said, getting up and crossing the room to place herself in his arms.

He smiled and touched her chin lightly before dropping a kiss upon her mouth. Wanting. There was something wanting. He should have been moved to passion. She took his hand and guided him to the cushioned settee by the window. There lay next to the sofa a satinwood table on top of which rested an open box.

60

He glanced at it absently but became intrigued when she quickly snatched up the card beside it and put it away.

"An admirer?" he asked on a cool note.

"I have them," she answered noncommittally.

He smiled amicably. "So you do, and I am among them."

"You are the only one who matters, love." She was very near to him now.

There was something about her this morning that he could not name, and it was disturbing the amorous mood he had arrived in.

"Francine . . ."

"Yes, love?"

Again he looked at her, and there was so much beauty there that it nearly blinded him to the expression in her eyes . . . nearly, but not quite. "Never mind . . . I only stopped by. . . ." He reached into his inner pocket and produced a small black velvet case.

She took it up eagerly. It opened to display a set of very fine sapphire earrings. She was disappointed. Diamonds. She felt she deserved diamonds. "How beautiful," she exclaimed dutifully and planted a kiss upon his cheek.

He got to his feet. His trouble had been for the last few years that he saw too much too clearly. "I must go. . . ."

"Oh . . . so soon, my love . . . can you not stay? Will you return today?"

"No, I can't stay, as I am engaged to meet some friends . . . and yes, perhaps I shall return later today."

She watched him go. Love? No, he did not love her, and she doubted that even she with all her wits, experience and charm could move him in that way. She had erred this morning. Somehow she had not pleased him. She would be more careful what she was about in the future, for he was not like other men. Never mind, she told herself, in the end it would not be affection that won him. She would have to devise a plan, entrap him with a scheme . . . it would take some doing . . . some investigating into his everyday life. This she would do, for she had every intention of becoming the next Lady Severn!

Mary picked up a gaudy piece of jewelry, smiled at its opulent design, and put it down. She felt the sleeve of her yellow pelisse pulled and she brushed at her companion with a sigh.

"Oh, do stop, Randy . . . I will come away in a moment."

"Faw!" was the answer she received. "These are shabby baubles, m'girl." He hesitated and then plunged on. "Come with me, Mary, and I'll take you to a first-rate jeweler where you might pick out *a diamond ring.* . . ." His eyes implored her to return the adoring look he cast her way.

She glanced up at that and away from the park peddler's wares.

"What did you say? Randy . . . what are you saying?"

He was in agony. For the life of him he did not really know what he was saying any more. He was blushing. He was perspiring. She was absolutely right. What was he doing? So, he did it again.

"Want . . . want you . . . to ma . . . marry me."

She perceived that Randall of Southvale was not himself. She could see that he was in quite a state, and so far from taking pity on him she burst into laughter, which completely served her purpose. He fired up at once.

" 'Tis nothing to laugh at. I daresay you could do worse!"

She took up his hand and held it to her cheek. "Dearest friend, I could do a great deal worse, but what is that to say? Don't you realize that if I were so foolish as to take your very obliging offer seriously I would be doing you an ill turn?"

"No, don't see that."

Severn was in the devil of a mood. Francine had not soothed his agitation. Instead, somehow she had added to it. Time and the wrong women had left him a cynic. The world looked very bleak, very cold, and as he tooled his team toward the park he was almost past caring. And then an interesting scene caught his eye. He saw Mary of Montlaine in close conversation with Southvale, a pup of a lad. He saw her laugh and hold Southvale's hand to her cheek, and he wondered if he had misjudged Mary. He had thought her an imp, an innocent, he had thought her a child. He saw now that she was capable of all a woman's wiles, and it irked him nearly into fury. He drove their way.

Mary looked up and saw Severn coming. "Hush

63

now, Randy, Severn will soon be upon us."

"No. Want an answer. A man proposes, deserves an answer."

"Very well then, my answer is no."

"Dash it, Mary, at least think about it."

"But Randy . . . you know that it is Richard I want."

"Don't know that at all . . . in fact . . ."

Severn tipped his hat toward Mary. "Good morning, Miss Montlaine . . ." He turned to her companion. "Southvale." He turned once more to Mary, and in spite of himself his expression softened, for there was such a look of sweetness about her. "How do you happen to be up and abroad already? I should have thought you would be flooded with callers this morning."

"No doubt you would, sir, for I believe you think you have brought me into style," she snapped at once.

He laughed. "Did it sound so? I never meant any such thing."

She relented. "Well, the sorry truth is that is precisely what you have done. I had morning callers enough before . . . now they parade through the house constantly, and I called to Randy here to rescue me."

"I see," he said dryly.

"Do you?" she returned coldly, for she disliked his tone. She did not know why he used it, but she put her chin well up as an indication that she would have none of it.

He let go a gust of laughter. "Come down from

the boughs, you little spitfire. I don't mean to do battle with you."

At that moment she was spared a retort, for she looked up to find Richard placing a languishing kiss upon Nina Clifford's gloved hand, whereupon she lifted her skirts and he helped her into a hack, gave the driver a short order and stood watching the vehicle make its progress before he turned and caught sight of his cousin, who stood a little apart from Mary and Severn and looked very much in the sulks.

"Hallo!" called Richard of Grey as he sauntered merrily their way. He fixed his cousin with a very speaking look and took his shoulder. "Deuced glad I've found you."

"Wasn't home," returned Randy, still very much in the sulks. "Was at your parents' . . . calling on Mary."

"Were you?" Richard sounded surprised but then brushed this aside. "Never mind that now, we have scarcely enough time to flag down a hack and make it over to Jackson's."

"Jackson's?" repeated Randy on a puzzled note.

"Never say you have forgotten?" Richard was much shocked. "Upon my soul, man, the black is fighting Molnieu today?" he turned to Lord Severn, perched above them in his phaeton. "Do you come, my lord?"

"I think not. . . . However, if Miss Montlaine should not mind it, I would be honored to drive her home and thus allow Southvale to accompany you."

"No," put in Randy. "Can't go."

"Can't go? Why the devil not? Excuse me, Mary, but this is beyond everything. Randy . . . ?"

"Must escort Mary home. Brought her out . . . take her home. Must see that," said Randy obstinately.

Mary had been quietly listening to all of this. Richard had been out strolling with Nina Clifford, but he was not so lost in love as to forego a pugilism match. It was an interesting observation. She patted Randy's hand. "You go on with Richard . . . I promise you I shall be very safe in Lord Severn's care." She turned a low aside to his lordship for no other reason except that she could not resist a tease. "Won't I?"

His eyes twinkled at her, but he was already taking her hand, pulling her up beside him. In a low tone meant only for her he said, "In this instance, my beauty, you will be safe enough in my hands. I won't, however, make it a promise for the future."

She arched her head. "Oh? I shall remember that, my lord."

They waved themselves off, and a moment later Mary was watching his lordship's skill with the ribbons, for the traffic had converged into a heated obstacle course.

Chapter Five

His lordship was for a time totally involved with his team and the bustling traffic; thus Mary was allowed a moment's reflection. It appeared to her that Richard was not at all in love with the Clifford woman. It appeared to her that what was needed was a game to make him aware of herself as a desirable woman. How? She so disliked dishonesty and love games, but what else could she do?

Make him jealous? It might answer. With whom could she consort without danger? Randy? No, he was too infatuated with her now, it would not serve, nor would any of the blades paying her court. Who? She looked at his lordship's profile, and suddenly her face beamed with the answer.

Severn happened to glance her way at that propitious moment, and his eyes twinkled appreciatively. "Good lord! What has thrown you into transports?"

"A fancy, my lord ... a fancy for you," she rallied.

"Oh? Do I detect a tease?"

"I suppose I shall have to be honest with you if I am to enlist your help."

"I suppose that is necessary, though I haven't promised to help you," he answered uncompromisingly.

She puckered up. "Now, you must give your word to keep my confidence whether you aid me or not."

"Very well, 'tis agreed." In spite of himself he was thoroughly intrigued.

She blushed, controlled herself and dove in breathlessly. "You see, for three years . . . I have been . . . I . . . well, I met Richard of Grey three years ago when he came to Montlaine with his sister, Vanessa."

"And you immediately became infatuated with the lad. Understandable," returned his lordship.

"More than that. I . . . I want to marry him."

"Do you?" His lordship felt a flutter in his breast, though why such an announcement should cause him any concern was more than he could fathom.

"Yes . . . but he fancies himself in love with Mrs. Clifford. Now, if she were right for him, which she is not, I would just leave matters as they are. . . ."

"But as she is not . . . ?" he urged.

"I would somehow turn his interest . . . *my way*."

"That should not be difficult."

"Oh, but it is. You see, Richard has gotten into the habit of treating me like a . . . a younger

68

relation . . . almost a sister. He doesn't realize I am quite grown-up."

"His cousin Southvale, however, does," said his lordship dryly.

"Yes, but he won't serve in this instance, because . . . well . . . never mind. It would be wicked of me to ask Randy to help me . . . while on the other hand . . . *you* would be perfect!"

"Would I?" said his lordship sweetly. "How so?"

"Well, if you were to show a marked preference for me . . . Richard would at first be concerned because . . . because of your reputation with women. After that . . . perhaps things might develop favorably between us."

"The age-old ploy. Jealousy? You are forgetting that Nina Clifford still holds his strings." He glanced at her frowning countenance. "Or do you mean to do away with her?"

"No . . . Nina Clifford has a great many admirers, hasn't she? If she were to get her back up . . . about Richard's spending time with me, which he would have to do if he wished to steer me away from you . . . well . . . one never knows. At least it would be action, which would be so much better than sitting back idly!"

"How marked must my attention be?" He had pulled up outside the double doors of the Greys' town house. One hand held the reins, the other slid round the back of her seat. His gray eyes appraised her face.

"Oh . . . just so . . . and whenever Richard is about," she returned with the glimmer of a smile.

He flicked her nose and laughed, and she cried out gleefully, "Excellent. I think you already have the hang of it."

He made her no promises, and when they parted she had no clear idea of how he would treat her request. It was outrageous, she told herself. What must he think of her? And so it was that his lordship, his reaction to her entreaty, the time he had spent at Montlaine when she had been a child and her present predicament held her thoughts as she lounged in her bath and made ready for Lady Grey's dinner that evening.

Randy and Richard exploded into the drawing room later that afternoon much flushed and spluttering with their news. The expedition, it seemed, had gone as they had hoped and they had come away much in the money because of their wise wagers. They preened and were inclined to be quite proud of themselves as they repeated anecdotes for Lady Grey's and Mary's entertainment. However, when Lady Grey casually reminded her son that she wished him to be present early enough to greet her dinner guests, he hemmed his way out of it.

"Oh, as to that, Mama . . . I shouldn't be too late. . . ."

Lady Grey's delicate brow went up. "Why . . . what should keep you?"

"Mean to escort, Mrs. Clifford, you know . . . she won't want to be the first arrival. Wouldn't be seemly . . . likes to make an entrance. . . ."

"Does she?" returned Lady Grey coldly, and

then, after a pause, "And you mean to make an entrance . . . with her?"

"Well . . . can't allow her to come alone . . . can I? Dash it, Mother . . . why shouldn't I escort her?" He was quick to line himself for defense.

She saw this at once and felt a pang of hurt. "Why indeed?" With which she got to her feet and abruptly left the room.

The remaining party watched the trail of her mauve silks and then exchanged glances. Richard frowned as they turned to stare at him.

"Well . . . what have I done? Devil take it . . . what has her nettled with me now?"

"No doubt, Richard, your mother wishes you on hand to greet her guests. They are, after all, for the most part some of your family's closest friends and relatives."

He eyed her for a long moment. She was looking fetching in her simple gown of pink muslin. There was a sweetness about Mary that would ever be appealing. More than that, he rather knew she was infatuated with him, and he considered her a good sport to step aside for the beautiful Nina Clifford. He reached out and touched her chin.

"Wise little Mary. . . . But in this instance, Mother will have to be disappointed."

"I see," she said quietly and watched him as he picked up his gloves and hat and motioned to his cousin.

"Do you come, Randy?"

"No . . . not yet, I think," returned his cousin.

"Well, I'm off then. See you later." And a moment later Richard of Grey had left them to eye one another.

Mary waited only for the closing of the drawing-room doors.

"You will, of course, go with him to take up Mrs. Clifford."

"What?" ejaculated Randall of Southvale. "Whatever for? I ain't one of her cicisbeos!"

"No, and none of them happens to be invited to this dinner. Randy, don't you realize how odd it would look for Richard to walk in with Nina Clifford at his mother's dinner? It is, after all, an intimate one. . . ."

Randall considered this. "Hmmm. It would appear singular in this instance . . . but . . ."

"But? There are no buts you can put forth that are worth a sou!" announced the lady hotly. " 'Tis the least you can do for your aunt."

"Well . . . if it is what *you* wish, Mary?"

"I do wish it, Randy, but I would think better of you if you wished it as well," retorted the lady.

He was her slave. There was nothing for it but to give in wholeheartedly. He became the champion of her cause, and forgotten was the fact that her cause was to win Richard of Grey.

"A glistening angel in white froth." Lord Sidmouth nodded and beamed as Mary flitted by throwing him an engaging smile. "Aye, that is what she is, Lady Grey, a veritable angel."

Indeed, thought Lady Grey, surveying her charge, she was that. Pearls and small diamonds glimmered around Mary's neck. Small white silk rosebuds sparkling with the same jewels peeped between the short, carefully disordered dark curls that framed her piquant face. White silk daintily embroidered with pearls clung alluringly to her form, and there was no doubt that Mary had captivated the assembled company.

A sound at the drawing-room door brought around Mary's head quickly, hopefully. Oddly enough it was not Richard she sought. Her hope was answered in the virile male form that stood on the drawing-room threshold, and she was momentarily diverted by her own heartbeat. Severn stood surveying the group. His russet hair sparkled with gold highlights beneath the candlelight. His shoulders seemed to fill the doorway. He wore a dark-grey velvet coat that exactly matched his eyes. His breeches clung to his athletic legs, his silk waistcoat gleamed white and was handsomely threaded with steel gray. His neckcloth was perfection. His Hessians shone, and from their heart-shaped tops swung silver tassels. He was in every way a Corinthian. Mary was hit by this fact most stunningly as he adroitly weaved his way toward her.

Lord Severn had come to this party with mixed emotions. Mary filled his thoughts. She was an engaging little minx. She was the sister of a good friend. She was sweet . . . and she was dangerous! To trust her was the question. His experience with women had not been good. They were usually selfish . . . fickle and sometimes quite cruel. It was hard to think of Mary that way . . . yet here she was saying she wanted Richard, but he had seen her in an earnest flirtation with South-vale that very morning. Who was to say she was not playing off one against the other?

Then too he knew himself to be a marriage prize. Perhaps she was trying to entrap him with a ruse. Employ him to pay her court publicly under the disguise of making Richard jealous when in the end she meant to bring not Richard but himself up to scratch. Dangerous! And then he looked across the room at her charming face and found himself moving toward her. He nodded to friends as he passed them, touched a shoulder here, there, smiled, and then he was taking up her hand, putting it to his lips.

"Mary, sweet Mary, shall you bear-lead me this evening?" His eyes twinkled with his tease.

She let go a laugh and clapped her hands together. "Then you mean to lend me your help, my lord?"

He nodded. "What choice do I have?"

"I daresay you have many, for I doubt I could whistle you to heel if you willed it otherwise."

"That is the point. I find I have no will of my own. I am yours to command."

"Famous! You are doing splendidly ... but do save it till Richard arrives."

It was his turn to laugh. "Don't you think I have enough quips to last the evening?"

She eyed him speculatively. "Hmmm. I am persuaded you must ... but we don't want to draw too much attention to ourselves all in one evening." She witnessed Nina Clifford's entrance with Randy and Richard flanking her sides. She pulled on Severn's sleeve. "My lord, *he* is here. You may start."

"May I indeed?" quizzed his lordship, turning to eye Nina Clifford's entrance. The widow was dressed in flaming red. It set off her yellow curls most strikingly. He put a finger thoughtfully to his nose and suggested idly, "You know, Mary . . . it might not be a bad notion if instead of dallying with you, I cut Richard out with Nina."

Mary frowned. "I thought of that. It won't serve. Richard might feel it necessary to call you out, and I don't want him hurt. . . . Besides, I don't think Mrs. Clifford would fall in with that scheme."

He was vastly entertained. "Don't you? Why not?"

"Because she means to wed Richard . . . and knows she won't get that prize from you. Now . . . don't stand there like a stock, sir, start dallying with me!"

It was not however until after dinner that Richard took notice of the fact that Severn was paying far more attention to Mary than he thought seemly, and it was Randall of Southvale that brought his attention to it.

"Don't like it, Richard," said Randy moodily.

"Eh? Don't like what, noddy?" returned his cousin affectionately.

"Severn . . . making Mary his prey!"

Richard looked wide-eyed at that. "No! He wouldn't dare!"

"Look at him. He was seated beside her at dinner . . . and has nearly been in her pocket all the evening. What's more, she has kept him laughing all the while. Ever known Severn to find a chit of Mary's cut amusing more than five minutes? Mark me, Richard . . . he means to seduce our Mary," asserted Randy testily.

Richard glanced toward Mrs. Clifford and satisfied himself that she was happily engaged in gossip with Lady Jersey, then set himself off in Mary and Severn's direction.

Mary looked up to find Richard descending on them. "Gracious, Severn, he is coming our way!"

"Is he? Damned impudent of him. Shall I send him off?"

She laughed and rapped his knuckles with her gilt-edged fan. "Don't you dare. Be nice, Severn . . . please?"

He sighed. "There is no sport in it. You know, Mary"—his voice dropped with his purpose—"you are far too small, far too soft, to wield such power over man." He flicked her nose. "Don't let it go to your lovely head. I shall not always be so pliable."

She beamed. "You are a dear."

"Am I? 'Tis not what you proclaimed me the other day."

"Well, you were most odious the other day. . . . Shh, now . . ."

"Mary!" called Richard. "So here you are." He nodded to Severn and then gave his full attention to Mary. "Been wanting a word with you, m'girl." He turned to Severn. "You don't mind . . . do you, my lord?"

"I do, but I can see that you are determined." Severn turned to Mary and took up her hand to his lips. "I shall leave you, sweet Mary . . . but trust you won't disappoint me tomorrow."

Mary smiled at him, and Richard waited only long enough to see Severn take leave of his mother before he took up Mary's arm and pulled her to a quiet corner.

"Mary! I can't believe it of you. After we had that talk . . . don't you know what Severn is?"

"Yes, of course. He is a friend of my brother's. He is also my friend."

"Some friend. He is turning you up sweet. Mary . . . he means you no good!"

"Really. You think he means to seduce me?" she asked with an arch look.

Richard frowned. "Well . . . it ain't in his line . . . never heard it said that he took on chits of your stamp . . . but . . ."

"But? But what? Perhaps he is far more interested in me than you imagine, Richard." She leaned away from him. "Look at me, Richard. I am child no more. . . ."

She was amused to find that he did indeed take careful stock of her. "Well, Richard?"

"By Jove, Mary . . . that's a fact, and all the more reason why I had best keep my eye on you. Now, what the deuce did he mean . . . asking you not to disappoint him tomorrow?"

"That is none of your affair. Do I bother you with questions about Nina Clifford? Do I?"

"Nooo . . . but that is different."

" 'Tis not. Now, if you don't mind . . ."

"Richard?" It was Nina Clifford.

He turned at once and stepped toward her. "A moment, Nina . . ."

"Richard . . . I want you to take me home," she returned, somewhat irritated to find him less responsive to her call.

"And so I shall, love . . . in a moment," returned Richard, for he had still a great deal to say to Mary.

Mary stood back and watched, vastly entertained and somewhat detached. In fact, she was far too detached for a girl in love, and this was a thing that struck her in that moment. She brushed it aside.

"I have the headache, Richard, and if you won't take me home this instant . . ."

He turned at that and gave her his full attention. "Very well, love . . . I'll have my carriage sent for." He frowned at Mary. "I will stop by tomorrow morning . . . for there is more I wish to say to you."

Mary smiled to herself and felt in that moment the evening had been a success.

Chapter Six

Severn wielded his team through the morning bustle and wondered why in heaven's name he had appointed himself to this task. Last night it had seemed the most natural thing in the world to invite the chit for a morning's ride ... but now, now he had his doubts.

Mary had kept him well enough entertained last evening, but girls of her age were prone to be missish. While he had not yet seen this lamentable trait in Miss Montlaine he worried lest he might and be heartily bored within five minutes of taking her up for this excursion. This was a new thing for him, putting himself out for a woman!

Ah well, she was after all the sister of Montlaine, and Montlaine was dear to his heart. Perhaps he could help her in her efforts with young Grey. And then Tootles, the Greys' butler, was opening wide the front door and Mary was descending the stairs before him and all doubts were cast aside. She was breathtaking.

She was beaming at him, and he was all too aware of her provocative lines in the aqua-blue habit she wore. It was delicately embroidered with white threading, and the design enhanced his observation that her waist would fit nicely in his grip. Dark curls whispered around her lovely face, adorned now with a confection of aqua blue and white tilted just so over her forehead. Her eyes were full of impish delight, and Severn had to slap himself silently. This was not the first beautiful chit he had come across, and it would not be the last. He went forward and took up her gloved hand. "Mary . . . you were made to break hearts!"

She raised her eyebrow with disapproval. "Oh! What a terrible thing to say to me!"

He regarded her in some astonishment. "Mary, I have just given you the compliment all women strive toward."

She wrinkled her nose. "No, I can't believe that to be so. There is not a heart I wish to break, and if I thought I had done so it would quite ruin my season."

He was leading her outside, setting her comfortably on the seat of his high-perch phaeton, motioning for the tiger to give him the reins, and still he managed to lean very near to her and say quizzically, "But Mary, is that not what you are attempting to do, break young Grey's heart?"

"Certainly not!" Her cheeks became flushed with her indignation. "There is a great deal of difference between winning a man's heart and breaking it."

"Is there? I have never discerned it," he answered dryly.

She regarded him thoughtfully a moment. "Ah, I see what it is now. Poor cynic. Some lovely creature sometime long ago hurt you very badly. You've been afraid to ever give another the opportunity to redeem our gender in your eyes."

His laugh was harsh. "Not at all. I am not afraid of forming an attachment, I am simply too supine for the rigors such an attachment would arouse."

"Oh, stop . . . there is a bitterness in you that did not develop because of apathy!"

His tone was curt when he answered, "Is that how I appear? Perhaps then it is because I draw my opinions from reality."

"How very odd that our realities should be so very far apart," she returned with a frown. "Which one of us is wrong, my lord?"

It was his turn to glance thoughtfully at her face. He regarded her much longer than he should have, so that she had to laugh and call his attention to the oncoming cart he was heading straight toward. He took it in good turn, tooled his team deftly out of the way and gave her his reply.

"Ah, Mary, your question deserves an answer, but since it wouldn't satisfy you now to have it from me, we'll leave it to time."

Chapter Seven

Denise Avery was by nature a timid creature with a softness of spirit that seldom balked at authority. It was not that she held no opinions of her own, for she did; it was simply that she realized the world she was allowed held no concern for her opinions.

Fate had orphaned her without a sou and put her in the household of her father's brother. There she had existed as a poor relation for a great many years, without the bitterness a spirited maid night have suffered.

There was too in Denise's character a sweetness of soul that enabled her to serve, fetch, tend and obey the caprices of her uncle and aunt with genuine gratitude. If she questioned their whims it was never voiced. If she dreamed of a different life, she did not allow those dreams to disturb the strength of her habitual mood of tranquillity. She derived a great deal of pleasure, amusement, solace and hope from the books that made up her private world. And then Mr. Felix Penistone intruded upon her peace.

Penistone was a middle-aged widower with a great deal of financial power, a growing quantity of political ambition and a keen eye for beauty. His background, his family ties, allowed him only to skirt society. Denise Avery with her bright-gold ringlets, her large blue eyes, her creamy-white complexion and sweetness of disposition was not only beautiful, she was quality. He watched her whenever he chanced to visit with George Avery, and he soon made up his mind to have her!

As of late, too often did Denise feel Penistone's pin-sized dark eyes follow her about. It made her uncomfortable. His smile repelled her. His words, whispered in low cunning tones, made her feel sick with dread. Instinct warned her, good sense patted her shoulder, fear sent her scurrying off whenever he was about the Avery house.

George Avery was not surprised when Penistone applied to him for Denise's hand. Here now was the opportunity to rid himself of a burden, for his children were off to school and he had not much need of her. There too . . . Penistone might be willing to settle an attractive sum on the girl.

It was an easy thing for George Avery to convince himself that he was making a splendid match for the girl. Speedily, satisfactorily, cunningly, it was decided between Avery and Penistone, and Denise Avery was sold from one bondage to another.

Denise had been for days nearly tiptoeing about

the house, afraid without knowing why. She sensed something to do with her was in the wind, and she wondered what it could be. Now and then she was struck by the dreadful fear, where would she go, how would she live, if her uncle and aunt were to turn her out?

Always she told herself that they would not. This was her father's brother. Her father had put her in his care, and her father had loved her. She had that memory, and still something in the household was afoot, but what?

The day came when she got her answer. George Avery came into the house rubbing his hands together in anticipation of the vast sum he would soon receive in exchange for his niece. She was at that moment descending the narrow stairs to the dark hallway below, and he looked up to find her.

"Denise. Come with me, child." His tone seemed festive enough, but this was so unlike him that it put her on guard.

She followed him to the drawing-room doors, allowed him to open the door and preceded him into the poorly decorated and undersized chamber.

"Sit, my girl. Go on ... take up that wing chair. I want to look at you when I give you the news."

She did as she was bid, but her large blue eyes contemplated him anxiously. What had he done? What had he done? She knew, she brushed the knowledge aside, for it was unthinkable. Cruel. He wouldn't. He was her uncle. Her father's brother. He could not use her so abominably.

Avery looked across at his niece, saw her youthful, undeniably lovely countenance and felt a swift pang of guilt. Penistone was both too old and too dissipated for such an innocent as this. Here was his brother's child. . . .

Greed beat such notions down. "Penistone . . . you have met him often enough here?"

"Yes, sir." Her heart was sinking. Something wicked was rising. She felt it shouting inside of her heart and she fought to overcome it. This was her uncle. He had taken her in, given her a home. . . .

"And you liked him well enough?" He avoided her eye. She had so much of her father in her. He moved away, put his hands behind his back and attempted to think of the money he would soon receive.

She studied his round face. A pudding face without character. Something inside her suddenly wanted to rail at him. She knew without a doubt what he was leading up to, and she could not answer.

"Well?" he pursued. "You like him, don't you?"

Afraid to offend, too well bred to criticize her uncle's associates, she nodded dully in the affirmative and watched as he clapped his hands together.

"Splendid! He has made an offer for you. The very best you will ever receive . . . considering your straitened circumstances . . . and I have snapped it up. Now, what do you say, my girl, eh?"

Married to Penistone. A huge bolt of lightning

came crashing over her head, slaying the knight who rode across her dreams. Married to Penistone? No ... please God ... no ... no. That wicked bubble that she had been fighting rose to the surface. She attempted to whip it into place. This was her uncle. He knew best. He was doing the best thing for her. She attempted to calm herself. "Uncle ... you ... you accepted?" In her eyes were traces of horror.

"Of course I did. Think of what your life will be. Jewels, clothing, horses ... a town house ... a country house. How could I refuse?"

"I ... Uncle ... please ... I cannot marry Mr. Penistone."

"What? What the devil do you mean, you can't marry him? Ungrateful brat! You will do as I say." He was becoming beet red. He was unused to having his will challenged by his niece.

"Uncle ...?" There was a large tear rolling down her cheek. Ungrateful? How could he so unjustly accuse her of that? All these years she had tended his children, staying up with them during the measles when no one else would go near the sickroom. All these years at their beck and call. Still, it sent shivers through her to balk against him. "Please, Uncle ... not ... not Mr. Penistone ..."

"Penistone has done you an honor. I am ashamed to hear you speak so. Why, you should be overjoyed. Go to your own quarters, my girl, where you may compose yourself and think better of this matter. The announcement will soon be sent to the newspapers, and Penistone himself will be here for dinner this evening. Yes, perhaps reflection on what is due to me, due to your aunt, is needed."

She stared at him for a full moment. No. He didn't care about her future. He never had. He was gaining from this. Hadn't he gained from her father's death? Hadn't there been a fund in her name that he had drawn upon as soon as she had turned eighteen? She had signed over what little competence she possessed. Where was that now? No! Nothing was due to him, and certainly not her soul!

She left the room and stood in the hall. She would not marry Penistone. Oh God, the thought made her tremble with revulsion. She allowed the wickedness to rear its hoary head and knew it for what it was . . . *independence,* she would have her independence. She would not marry Penistone. Without a cloak, without hat, gloves or the benefit of a ha'penny, she ran to the front door, flung it open and sped outdoors!

Down the corner she ran as though a pack of dogs were at her heels. No, no, no. She would not, could not marry Penistone. She fled past peddlers, past young bucks ready to ogle and call out entreaties for her to linger. She ran and she ran, and when she finally stopped she knew she had only one last hope. *Nina Clifford!*

Chapter Eight

"Oh, do let us walk down this alley, my lord. Lady Grey never takes me to any but the best shops, and I would so like to see some of the quaint little stores I have heard so much about," pleaded Mary as she took up Severn's gloved hand and tugged.

She was captivating. It had flitted through his mind more than once that she was wholly absorbing, and though he did not relinquish his air of apathy he was vastly entertained in her company. It was, he told himself, because she was different and he was amused by her liveliness, nothing more.

"Mary, this is really too bad of you. Not only must you drag me to see Elgin's miserable marbles, but now you want to pull me through the filth of London? I must think myself hardly used."

She giggled. "They aren't miserable marbles. They are Athenian marbles rescued, I am told, from lime-burners in the Aegean, and at some cost as well as danger too!"

"Ah, is that what that impudent dog was telling you when I was fetching you a lemonade? Hmph! Danger indeed. May heaven preserve us from such wanderers who must needs explore every classical nook digging up the poor remains of Greece and Egypt, which they must then purchase in its weight in gold, pack up and ship home in addition to a Grecian temple or two as though they were no more than a few pieces of china. No, sweet Mary, such things hold no lure for me, nor, I am sure, do they for you."

"How can you say so? I liked them very well," she countered.

"How can I say so? My sweet, I derive my opinion from the speed with which you did the tour of poor Elgin's marbles," he said triumphantly.

She laughed out loud and conceded him a hit when something brought her up short and called all her attention. She put out her hand and held tight to Lord Severn's. *Someone was in trouble just ahead!*

Denise was not sure how she would find Nina Clifford. Nina was Denise's maternal aunt, but she had seen her only twice in the last ten years. Nina had been only a girl herself and quite unable to take charge of an orphaned child . . . but now perhaps she might lend her shelter, at least until a suitable post as governess might be found. It was Denise's only hope. She hailed a hackney.

"Eh?" The driver looked her over closely. No cloak, no hat, what was this?

"Please, sir . . . I am looking for the Clifford house . . . Mrs. Nina Clifford? Would you know just how I might find it?"

"Surely now, miss . . . hop in and I'll be taking ye there." He smiled to himself. There would be some money in this. All he had to do was deliver her to Mad Jack. . . .

Denise watched the passing scene. The parks and fashionable streets disappeared. Official-looking brick buildings came into view and then passed. Something was wrong. He was not taking her to her aunt's house. She had read just enough of Mrs. Radcliffe's novels to give her a lively imagination. She was stormed with a dirge of gruesome fears and called anxiously to the driver to stop. He did not seem to hear. However, an altercation in the traffic brought the vehicle to a slow enough speed for her to jump out. This she did, scurrying down the street and through the mouth of a cobblestoned alleyway.

This produced a series of connecting alleys, and as she rounded the corner she went full force into the belly of a large and rather dirty individual. He held her at arm's length.

"Lordy . . . what 'ave we 'ere?" He appraised her, and when it filtered into his gin-soaked brain that she was a yella-haired wench worthy of his attention, his grip tightened.

"Let me go!" cried Denise, near to hysterics now. This was fast turning into a nightmare of ghoulish proportions. Her mind chastised, see what comes of giving into evil rebellious inclinations? See where you have plunged yourself? "Let me go . . . please, let me go."

Mary heard the cry and looked up in time to see a large and questionable individual manhandling a pretty girl her own age. Immediately and without question she would have run to the fore, but Severn checked her progress, placing her behind him and taking over with aplomb.

"I think, sir, you might find me less to your liking but very much more your size!" said Severn, laying a hand on the man's shoulder.

The man spun around, making a guttural sound as he brought up his fists. However, this forward action won him a thudding blow to the center of his belly. Another followed upward, landing him a stiff facer that sent him reeling backward. His eyes opened wide, for he perceived that he had not been altogether wise in taking on this broad-shouldered nonesuch. Severn was moving menacingly toward him, and rather than encounter another blow the ruffian took off, flinging abuse over his shoulder and promising to return with his friends.

"Oh, that was very good of you, my lord! Famous!" cried Mary approvingly before turning her attention to the girl, who stood with her face in her hands. "Oh, no . . . do not cry. It is all over now. Lord Severn has made short work of that bully. Are you hurt? Poor thing . . . you are shivering." Mary patted the taller girl's hand but called to his lordship, "My lord . . . your cloak, please."

He had already removed it, was already handing it over when he received the command. Graciously he put it into her hand with a smile and a bow. Funny little managing thing, he thought, pluck to the backbone. What would she have done had he not been on hand? She would have flown at the ruffian, that's what she would have done. Incredible little chit. He felt a growing and rather reluctant sense of admiration as he watched Mary do her work.

"May I suggest," he put in gently, "that we leave the alley behind us?"

"Yes indeed," agreed Mary. "That dreadful man said he would return with his friends . . . though that doesn't signify . . . but Severn, they might have weapons!"

He twinkled at her, for there was no hiding the fact in this pronouncement that she thought him rather capable and that it would take a number of deadly weapons to do him in. He led her and the protesting maid toward the main road, where his tiger was attending his team and phaeton.

"But please . . . I can't impose myself on you," cried Miss Avery feebly.

"Nonsense. You are in some sort of 'trouble, and we would be paltry creatures indeed if we did not extend a hand." Mary turned to Severn. "Isn't that so, my lord?"

His lordship had it on the tip of his tongue to deny this, but the inquiring dark eyes Mary held up to him totally unmanned him. All they needed to do was to put the young woman in a hackney, but no, sweet Mary would frizzle up at such a suggestion. Meekly he allowed it to be so and thus incurred Mary's sunshine.

A moment later he had seated the ladies, jumped up beside Mary, found the fit rather more than snug, taken up the reins from his surprised tiger and sent his horses into a forward motion.

"Now, Miss . . . ?" started his lordship not unreasonably.

"Miss Avery . . . Denise Avery," supplied the frightened maid.

"Miss Avery . . . where shall we take you?"

She frowned, sighed, and cried, "I . . . I have been trying to find Mrs. Nina Clifford. If you would be so good as to inquire after her address for me . . . ?"

"Nina Clifford?" ejaculated Mary in some surprise. "*You* are looking for Nina Clifford?"

"Why, yes . . . you see, she is my aunt," said the girl on a frown. "Do you . . . are you acquainted with her?"

"Yes . . . yes . . . we are," said Mary, appraising the girl again. Upon closer scrutiny she could see that there was indeed a family resemblance. She turned to Severn. "I fancy you know Mrs. Clifford's direction?" There was a tease in her voice.

He glanced at her sharply and under his breath replied, "Minx! As a matter of fact . . . I do."

Mary twinkled at him and returned her attention to Miss Avery, taking up her hand. "How is it you do not know your aunt's whereabouts? And if it is none of my affair, feel free to tell me, I shan't take offense."

She smiled at Mary. "Oh, no . . . in spite of the

state in which you found me today, I am not so ill mannered. You see ... I haven't been in touch with my aunt since her marriage eight years ago."

"Ah ... but it was imperative that you reach her today?" pursued Mary gently.

The girl gulped. "Yes ... yes ... something made it impossible for me to remain ... where I was ... and I have no one else. There is only Aunt Nina."

Mary wanted to know more, for these words tantalized her curiosity, but she kept her questions in check. She wasn't going to badger this poor girl.

Richard of Grey eyed Nina Clifford ardently as she sipped at her morning coffee. She was devastatingly alluring in the black dishabille she had chosen to don for his inevitable morning call. He wanted to possess her. He wanted to touch her, to call her his own. Yes, there were things she did that irked him now and then. No, they did not think alike on many subjects ... and some of her fancies, in fact, rather shocked him ... but never mind, these were meaningless fripperies. Here was the woman he wanted.

He took a tour of the room, plucking himself up for the moment. He felt a nervous sweat begin to permeate his being. What was wrong? Here was the woman of his dreams. Go to her ... tell her, ask her. ...

She watched his agitation in some glee. He was about to propose. He displayed all the signs of a devoted puppy. She did not love him, but he

95

would elevate her one day to countess, for he was heir apparent to an earldom! His fortune too would keep her nicely, and when his vigilance cooled she would again take on her retinue of men. "Come, Richard . . . what is wrong?" she cooed.

He spun around and called her name. She patted the sofa cushion near where she lounged. He took long heavy strides in that direction and went down on one knee. Her hand was in his, clasped strongly, and he bent to place a fevered kiss upon her wrist.

"Nina . . . Nina darling . . ."

The door at his back opened wide, and a thin, small butler stood rigidly against it. "Miss Denise Avery, Miss Mary of Montlaine and Lord Severn."

Richard of Grey flushed and jumped to his feet. A proposal of marriage was glued thickly to his lips, and he felt all the embarrassment of a proud young man. "What is this? Are they expected, Nina?"

In some annoyance she stood up, the black lacy gown flowing to her dainty feet. It was infuriating. Richard had been at the very point of asking her to marry him. Oh, she could scream. She controlled herself, for Mary was already dragging in Miss Avery by the hand, and Severn could be seen at their backs.

"Oh, Mrs. Clifford . . . how glad I am that you are at home. Here is your niece, whom Severn has only moments ago rescued from the hands of a tallow-faced ruffian!" announced Mary of Montlaine. "Richard . . . hallo, you here? Only fancy, Richard, there was this monstrously large horrid man . . . but Severn merely landed him a blow to his breadbox, then up, up to his face, and planted him backward." She turned proudly toward Severn. "He was absolutely wonderful!"

Richard's eyes opened wide at this. "What? Mary . . . where have you been? What is this? Did some rum-touch attack you, Mary? For if so I shall have his head!"

"Well, the oaf didn't attack me, but poor Miss Avery here, and Severn has already had his head!"

"Look, Mary . . . you've got me all at sea. I wish you would start at the beginning!" complained Richard. A glance at Severn's countenance caused him to flush, for he could see the nonesuch found all this vastly entertaining.

"At the beginning, Richard?" Mary was in the mood to tease. "Well then, sir, as you wish it. Severn came around this morning to take me up for a ride in his perch phaeton. It wasn't long afterward that he was so very obliging and took me to see the Elgin Marbles, and only fancy, Richard—"

"Hold just a moment, Miss Montlaine!" interrupted Mrs. Clifford, and it was clear to the assembled company that she was in the devil of a temper. She turned on her niece. "Now, young lady, kindly explain how you happen to be in such a state!"

Miss Avery trembled. This was going to be much more difficult than she imagined. The Nina Clifford she had remembered was so different, so soft, so young. This one was not much older . . . but so very hard. There was nothing to do

97

but to plunge into the very heart of the matter.

"I have run away from my uncle's house," she said on a whisper.

"You what?" shrieked Mrs. Clifford. She was not going to be saddled with this beautiful chit. Her style of life would not allow it.

Miss Avery nearly fainted. Mary steadied her. "Hush. There is no reason to shout, Mrs. Clifford. It accomplishes little, and your niece has been through an ordeal."

Richard quite approved of this. "Yes, Nina dearest . . . I am certain your niece has good reason . . ." He turned to Miss Avery. "Don't you, child?"

Miss Avery gulped and nodded her head. "Oh, yes . . . yes."

"What is it, then?" demanded Mrs. Clifford.

Miss Avery twisted her fingers around in her agitation. "I shan't go back. I would rather die first."

Mary gave her shoulders a squeeze. "There now, Miss Avery, what has overset you? Perhaps we may be of some service?"

Miss Avery glanced across at Mary gratefully. "You have already done so much. I will sound a terrible girl . . . but I could not bring myself to . . . to . . ." A sob escaped.

Mary urged her on. "To what, Miss Avery? Did your uncle ask you to do something you could not like?"

Miss Avery nodded vigorously. "He wanted me to marry . . . a very rich man . . ."

Mrs. Clifford let go an exasperated oath. "Famous! You run away because your uncle settles a match I am sure you don't deserve."

"Did you not like this rich man?" Mary questioned gently.

Miss Avery shook her head. "No . . . I . . . he frightens me . . . and . . . I won't marry him."

"I am certain you can know nothing of the man," returned Nina Clifford. "It was probably handled roughly . . . your aunt should have been the one to talk to you." She was pacing the room. "How Avery could have been so clumsy . . ."

"Who is the man?" asked Richard curiously.

"Felix Penistone," supplied Denise on another sob.

"No!" ejaculated Richard. "Why, he is a skirter . . . and old enough to be your father!" Clearly he was shocked.

Mary glanced toward Severn and saw that he too found this piece of information disgusting. She then turned to Nina Clifford and was surprised to find her taking another side altogether.

"Felix? Why . . . what is wrong with poor Felix? I happen to know him well. He will make you an excellent husband."

Richard turned a troubled countenance on his love. "But Nina . . . no, you cannot mean that. The man is a roué . . . past his prime . . ."

"Richard! I am certain that if he wishes to remarry after all these years of being a widower, he means to leave such activities behind. I am certain he will make my niece an excellent husband."

"No! He is a terrible man and I won't marry him," announced Miss Avery. "He is forever licking his lips in the most odious fashion, and . . . and besides . . . I don't love him."

"Love? What has that to say to anything?" demanded Mrs. Clifford.

Mary watched Richard as he observed his love. Her brow went up appreciatively and she allowed Richard to answer her.

"Nina, dearest . . . I should think *you* would know that love has nearly everything to do with a good marriage. Do you want your niece to be unhappy?"

Mrs. Clifford shot her sweetheart a look to freeze. "I find your question insulting, Richard."

"Do you? It was not meant to be." Richard was flushing to the roots of his fair hair.

"It doesn't matter, at any rate, for Denise must be returned to her uncle, who is, I might add, her guardian."

"I won't go . . . and he is no longer my guardian! That ended when I turned eighteen . . . some months ago."

"I won't harbor you here, Denise. It would not be right. Your uncle must be very worried about you."

All this was very new to Denise Avery. All her life she had obeyed without demur. Suddenly she was making her own decisions, standing up to authority. It was uplifting.

"Perhaps, then, Aunt Nina . . . you will allow me to stay but a night until I can make suitable arrangements . . ."

"No, and I am surprised you should ask it of me. You will return immediately to your home and set your uncle's mind at ease," retorted Nina, furious with the girl for referring to her as aunt. It made her feel so old.

Mary pinched Denise's arm. "Miss Avery ... let us not trouble your aunt any further. Come, we will return you to your uncle's house."

"Oh, but ..." started Miss Avery and was quickly pinched again. She looked deep into Mary's dark eyes.

"Trust me," whispered Mary.

Richard took a step forward. "This is preposterous! I can't believe that you are sending this poor girl into Penistone's clutches!"

Nina put up her chin. "I think, Richard, that you had better leave." It was an error on her part. She bit her lip as soon as she observed Richard's expresson. She had embarrassed him before Severn. She had shocked him with her unfeeling display toward her niece. It all had happened so quickly. She would have to make a recovery ... but not now. He was in a temper and would not be soothed. Better to whistle him to heel later. Such were her thoughts as she watched the assembled company depart.

Chapter Nine

Outside the door Severn leaned very close to Mary and whispered in her ear, "You are, of course, a minx . . . but quite magnificent. What now do you propose to do with Miss Avery?"

She twinkled up at him and sucked in her lips with her thoughts, and as this caused him to burst into laughter she reprimanded him severely, "Hush, now . . . you will learn soon that I am quite resourceful." She turned to Miss Avery. "We have, you know, two courses open to us."

"No . . . no . . . you have already done so much for me . . . I cannot . . . will not trouble you further," cried Miss Avery.

Mary gazed at the pale lovely before her. Miss Avery appeared in need of bolstering. "Stuff! Shall we walk away and leave you with Severn's cloak about your shoulders?"

Miss Avery flushed and looked as though she were once again about to burst into tears. Mary took her shoulders. "Stop it, now. I asked you to trust me, and you came away from your aunt's on that promise. Why don't you just leave matters to me?"

"Oh, well, that is fine talking . . ." put in Richard in some agitation. His love had behaved badly. Here was this innocent and ethereal being reduced to tears, in fear for her future, and his dearest heart had not offered her even one night's shelter. It was really too bad of Nina and made him all the more determined to help the girl. "But Mary . . . just what do you intend for Miss Avery?"

Mary did not answer him but turned to Severn. "Gracious me, we should not be standing about in the street . . . and with your prime blood champing at their bits. Severn . . . would you escort Miss Avery and me home?"

Severn's eyes opened wide. "With great pleasure, my Mary."

"Home? You mean to take Miss Avery to Mama?" ejaculated Richard on a note of astonishment.

"You may follow us, Richard . . . for you won't fit in Severn's phaeton," offered Mary as she allowed Severn to lead her to his vehicle.

Richard stood a moment in stupefaction and then called after her, "I'll be dashed if I won't follow," with which he went about the business of hailing a hackney.

Once seated—in actuality crushed against Severn, for a high-perch phaeton was made for two passengers only—Miss Avery got up the courage to speak.

"Miss Montlaine . . . ?" she started.

"Mary," put in Miss Montlaine with a smile. "Please do call me Mary, and I shall call you Denise."

"Mary . . . you said you had two courses to follow . . . with regards to my immediate future. Would . . . could you perhaps tell me what you had in mind?"

"Aha!" Severn was moved to utter. "Do make her tell!"

Mary sent a quelling look his way but noted that it only served to make him grin. She restrained the bubble inside her throat, refrained from gurgling and addressed herself to the question at hand. "Well, I really didn't want to get into both roads until one had been explored. It is my intention to present you to Lady Grey, to be candid with her about your circumstances and to ask her to house you until a plan can be devised for your future."

"Oh . . . I could not . . . Lady Grey is a stranger . . . I could not . . ." cried the girl in some agitation.

"No, *you* could not ask such a thing of Lady Grey, for she is a stranger to you. However, she is no stranger to me. Her daughter is married to my brother, you see . . . and you are my friend and my guest. She is the best of good women . . . you will see. She will make no objection, and if she does, I shall send you to Montlaine."

Miss Avery sat back to digest this. This morning seemed an age ago. So much had happened. Her well-ordered, dull life had been turned havey-cavey. "I . . . I can only thank you, Mary. . . . Were it not for you . . ."

"Stuff! Ah ... here we are." She turned to Severn. "You needn't escort us inside. You have been very obliging ... and I am very grateful ... for everything."

He took up her hand and held it a moment before putting it to his lips. "So I am dismissed?"

"It would be better if I were to speak to Lady Grey alone." She dimpled at him. "You would, I am persuaded, be heartily bored anyway."

He laughed and said for her ears alone, "Mary, you have managed to keep me at the edge, wondering what next you will plunge me into. No ... I would not be bored. I think you are dismissing me for reasons all your own."

Some moments later found Mary closeted with her ladyship in the garden tea room. Lady Grey put down her volume of Jane Austen and contemplated her young charge. Something was afoot.

"No, of course you do not interrupt me," answered Lady Grey graciously, since it was obvious that Mary had indeed interrupted some very enjoyable reading.

"Oh, I know that I do ... and am heartily sorry for it, ma'am, for I also know you are so busy these days you rarely get a moment to put your feet up ... but 'tis terribly important."

"Of course it is. Now sit down beside me, love, and tell me what has you in such a state."

Mary sat on the edge of the settee and cast aside her gloves.

" 'Tis complicated, ma'am. . . . Severn and I rescued this girl ... she was being attacked by this monstrous man, and Severn sent him flying. Well, he threatened to come back with friends, and so we took Miss Avery and flew . . ."

"Miss Avery?"

"Yes, and wait till you hear, for she is Nina Clifford's niece . . ."

"Nina Clifford! Good gracious."

"Yes, and she was escaping her paternal uncle who was her guardian but isn't any more and Mrs. Clifford wouldn't give her sanctuary and Richard was there and thought very poorly of Mrs. Clifford for I could tell and so could she for she nearly froze him with a glance and then asked him to leave and well, I brought Miss Avery here . . . and please, ma'am . . . won't you let her stay . . . for just a while at least . . . until we can find a suitable arrangement for her?"

Lady Grey blinked. Her own daughter, Vanessa, had been a volatile, restless and headstrong minx. She had kept their household in a continual whirlwind, and they had sustained her antics. She was not therefore as bowled over as another mother might have been by Mary's laconic speech. She gathered that Mary had found a friend who in some way involved Nina Clifford. She shook her head and patted Mary's hand.

"Why don't you tell me all this less concisely? Stick in a detail or two and then perhaps I might be able to give you an answer."

Richard opened wide the drawing-room doors. Miss Avery stood in the chamber's center and made in spite of her dowdy brown day gown quite a pretty picture among the apple-green decor. Her long golden hair flowed down her neck and over her shoulders, her blue eyes were wide with his entrance, and he was immediately struck by her angelic appearance.

"Tootles told me you were in here."

In spite of the day's harrowing events, Miss Avery found it possible to giggle. "Tootles? How appropriate for a butler."

Richard grinned and put out his hand, indicating a chair. "Please, Miss Avery, do make yourself comfortable. I have sent for refreshments, and they should be here any moment." He was acutely aware that his beloved Nina had not even offered her niece a cup of tea. He frowned and took a turn about the room. "Mary is, I suppose, closeted with m'mother." It was more a statement than a question.

She nodded, took a long breath, sat down and brought up her serenely soft blue eyes to his face. "I am . . . so sorry to intrude upon all your lives in this . . . outlandish manner. What you must think of me. . . ." She turned her face away in hot confusion.

He went to her at once, sat down beside her and brought her chin around, forcing her to look at him. "Slap up to the echo! That's what I think of you. Why, you have courage, Miss Avery, a courage few girls in your circumstances possess."

She released a nervous laugh. "No . . . my aunt was clearly shocked with my rebellion."

He stiffened. "You were quite right for leaving your uncle's house . . . though," he continued and smiled at her quizzically, "next time you find it necessary to depart in haste, I would caution you to bring whatever garments you have handy." He waited for her answering smile and continued, "There too, Severn was correct in milling down the brute who dared to accost you, and Mary was acting correctly when she brought you to your aunt. So you see. All things have moved exactly as they should have done."

She allowed him a half-smile. "Aunt Nina thinks I have returned to my uncle's home."

Again the frown pulled his brows together. "Your aunt acted, I believe, in the strictest propriety . . . though I must own, what was needed was compassion, not propriety. Why, the very notion of *you* and Penistone is revolting!"

She sighed, pleased to find someone who fully entered into her feelings. "Still . . . I am deceiving my aunt . . . for which I am sorry, but I cannot go to my uncle and I cannot marry Penistone."

"You know . . . this uncle of yours. Is he queer in his attic?"

She giggled. "He is not. Whatever makes you ask such a thing?"

"Well, it ain't quite the thing to match you with a man like Penistone. I mean . . . well, if Penistone were a duke . . . or something . . . but good Lord, girl . . . the man is a skirter. What can your uncle be thinking of? It's a misalliance if ever there was one!"

She blushed. "It is a matter of finances. My uncle is not . . . well . . . not quite in the suds . . .

but I am a poor relation, you see . . . my circumstances are such that . . . that my dowry is but a pittance."

"Selling you off, is he? Your uncle sounds a rum touch to me."

"Oh, no . . . he has been quite good to me . . . he took me in . . . when my parents died."

"Oh, and what was he supposed to do, turn you off? I don't think so. No doubt you came with something of an inheritance that he has since claimed was needed for your support over the years?"

"Well, yes . . . but that would be perfectly true."

"Ha!" snorted Richard.

They were at that moment prevented from further discussion by the tea tray. As Miss Avery had not eaten a thing all day, she gave herself over with some relish to the plate of cakes and sweetmeats that met her eye. Richard watched her as he sipped his sherry and set himself to thinking.

The doors were opened wide a moment later to emit Mary and Lady Grey. Happily Mary almost skipped to Miss Avery, took up her hands and told her gleefully, "Do you see? Now everything will be settled right and tight."

Miss Avery was reduced to stammering blushes before her ladyship was introduced, but Mary's lively manner soon set them all at ease. A period of questions and answers followed before all concerned fell into easy conversation.

Severn headed his team homeward. Mary was

beginning to play much too much with his thoughts. He suspected himself of being far too attracted by the spirited maid. No, Severn, he told himself, don't do it . . . never allow yourself to think them better than what they are. Love? It always dies in the end. Men and women claw at one another until there is nothing left. He shook his head ruefully. She is just a passing fancy. It was then that a familiar figure caught his eye.

Francine White stood in splendid array. For a moment one might even take her for a duchess, so well did she carry off her style. It was really too bad how grasping she was, how she could not even disguise it any more from him. Beside her stood a gentleman whose fashion depicted him a man of questionable means. They seemed caught up in one another's conversation, and to Severn's percipient eye the couple were passing more, much more, than the simple amenities.

Up went Severn's brow. It was interesting, for he wondered what Francine had to do with such a man. He had not been to visit her since that morning, and he had not responded to her letter of yesterday. As he pulled up his team she turned her lovely golden head with its huge pink flowered silk hat.

"Severn!" she exclaimed in some surprise, and then quickly recovered. An odd expression descended over her features. "But darling, where is the little pretty you were escorting all about town this morning? Did you tire of her already?"

He showed no surprise. Obviously she had seen him with Mary. It rather nettled him to hear her refer to Mary in such terms, but he brushed this consideration aside. What did matter was that Francine needed a sharp set-down, for apparently she seemed to feel she had a claim on him.

"As you are not acquainted with the lady to whom you refer, I cannot comprehend why her whereabouts should interest you." With this he nodded and meant to depart. However, she stayed him hastily.

She was furious, but she attempted to win him over. "What interests me is the answer to my question."

"Which question is that, Francine?"

"The one I asked you in my note yesterday. Do you come to see me soon?"

He studied her a moment. His eyes flickered over the man at her back, and he felt a wave of pity, for the fellow seemed gravely affected by this scene. She was a heartless jade. "No, Francine, I think not."

Open-mouthed, she watched him drive away. Plague take his soul! Hard-hearted fiend! So, he was ending it, was he? So, he would have none of her, eh? No, Severn. Not so easily. She voiced her feelings.

"I shall make him sorry, Tom . . . I swear it!"

"Will ye, love?" The dark-haired gypsy at her side turned her chin his way. "How would the likes of ye be doing sech a thing to a lord?"

"I don't know at this moment . . . but Tom, I shall find a way to make him pay, for he has ill served me."

"Lass . . . Lass . . ."

"No, you know by now that I have always attained what I strived for."

"Aye, ye can talk flash with the quality ... sound like 'em ... look like 'em ... but Francie, love ... ye ain't one of 'em ... and they'll only hate ye for squeezing in on their game!"

"No! One day I will marry into a name ... into a family. I have to, Tom ... you understand, don't you?"

"Lord, woman ... I've known ye, loved ye, too long not to understand, but ye be heading for heartache."

"No ... I am not. Not a one in this world ... not even you ... can hurt me, Tom. I was past that a long time ago."

"Right, then. Forget Severn. . . ."

She smiled and touched the man's cheek. He was her Tom. She was at home with him, herself with him, and even he did not know the depths her hatred could travel. "Forget? Oh, no ... he has served me in such a way I shan't ever forget. I promise you, Severn will not come out of this unscathed. One way or another I shall find the means to hurt him."

He put his arm about her. "Love, love ... it's me ye'll love till yer dying day. We be two alike. . . ."

She sighed and stroked him. " 'Tis a truth, poor Tom, but I can't marry you. I want more ... so much more."

"Well, ye won't be getting it from Severn."

"Oh? Don't you think so? Well, we shall see."

Chapter Ten

The Greys' formal dining room was styled in the highest kick of fashion. Its rich furnishings of gold and brown were Regency in design and certainly in the first elegance. Its size was large, its artifacts varied and rare, and yet its touch was warm, inviting and full with family character. One felt immediately comfortable without any discernible cause. An enormous fireplace dominated the far wall and was now crackling merrily to the tune of lively conversation.

Miss Avery scanned her surroundings and her companions and felt momentarily moved to tears. Such was her gratitude toward the Greys and Mary. There was no obvious effort to make her feel at ease, and yet she did and she knew it was all their doing. Lady Grey had swept in upon Mary and her that afternoon holding a quantity of gowns.

"These were Vanessa's, and you must know, my dear, that since she was married three years ago she won't wear them. Insists they are too missish, which is quite ridiculous, as my Nessie never wore a missish thing ever . . . but . . ." She held up a lovely silk of bright blue to Denise's figure. "Ah . . . yes, a tuck here and there . . . and an inch or two at the hemline, for Ness is not much taller than our Mary here . . . yes, indeed, these will do nicely." She ignored Denise's blushing protest and swooped up a simple but magnificent gown of pink and white. "This style should fit you for tonight . . . until the others can be fitted to your figure. Now, I must run, as Lady Jersey and I are promised to Lady Sefton for high tea." With that she had been gone.

"Mary . . . I cannot accept these things," cried Denise in some agitation as Lady Grey vanished in a swish of skirts.

"Stuff! Why the deuce can't you?"

"It would be grossly improper. However could I repay her? I am already so much in her debt."

"Oh, fiddle. Nessie will never wear those things again. My brother provides for her, let me tell you, and she would never grudge you these clothes. Dennie . . . I mean to present you to the polite world . . . oh, not in a grand way . . . but just enough to put Nina Clifford's nose out of joint. You see, she means to marry Richard."

"Oh, no . . ." breathed Denise and then blushed hotly. "I . . . she is my aunt . . . I could not do anything that would hurt her."

"Oh, pooh! She didn't give a fig for your comfort all these years. You don't owe her a thing. She means to marry Richard, and Dennie, I must tell you, though she is your blood relative . . .

well, it is not the sort of marriage for Richard."

Denise Avery frowned. "She is very beautiful . . . and Mary . . . I do believe she is good ton . . . I know I have heard my Uncle Avery often say so."

"She is also far too sophisticated for Richard . . . and what is more to the point, Dennie, she does not love him."

"Then why . . . why do you think she will marry him?"

"Well, who wouldn't? He is heir apparent to an earldom and a fortune . . . he is sweet, good . . . handsome . . ."

"Yes," agreed Miss Avery simply.

Mary studied her a moment and then was about to say that she intended to win Richard for herself. Inexplicably she refrained, and instead they began exchanging tales of their childhood.

Denise sighed to herself as she remembered the pleasantness of the afternoon. Even meeting the earl had been an easy thing. She had worried about the moment when she would be introduced, but upon finding herself facing him just before dinner, he had smiled and said jovially how pleasant it was to have his house full of beautiful children, whereupon he had excused himself and gone off to his club. She glanced around the oval table. Was this all a dream? Would she wake up once again in her uncle's home?

No, not a dream. Here was Richard of Grey, jabbing at his food and debating hotly with Mary over some nonsense. It seemed that he and Mary were forever at odds over something or other, and yet she could see they were very fond of one

117

another. Lady Grey presided over the meal, and Denise could see that the countess was pleased to have her son taking dinner with them. Only one thing, a question, kept rearing. What of tomorrow? What would happen then? Because there was no answer, she sighed.

Mary heard her friend's almost inaudible release and immediately touched Miss Avery's hand. "You are bothering your head again, and Dennie, I have told you I won't have it. Really, girl, it shows a deplorable lack of confidence in me."

Denise smiled apologetically. "It is just that you refuse to discuss what really should be done with me."

"Done with you?" interjected Richard. "What do you mean, done with you? Mary told me earlier that she had it settled all right and tight." He turned on Mary. "Didn't you tell me that?"

"Yes, and so I have, Richard."

"Well then . . . why don't Miss Avery here know about it, Mary?"

"She does, but she is being difficult."

"What do you plan doing with her?" pursued Richard and glanced toward his mother, who was noticably quiet.

"Well, I mean to launch her."

"Launch her? Devil a bit . . . will that do?"

"Well, yes, for I don't mean to do it in the grand style . . . but she will come into society with us. Isn't that so, ma'am?" said Mary in her way.

"Of course. I should meet no difficulty procuring invitations for a daughter of the house of

118

Avery. It is a good name," answered Lady Grey, watching her son.

He frowned. This would embarrass his beloved Nina. He had not seen Mrs. Clifford since the morning's affair, and he had not yet cooled off regarding her treatment of her niece and himself. Yet . . . ?

"No, no," said Denise. "If only you would consider the consequences, Mary . . . my lady." She put her hands together. "My uncle would be furious . . . he would, I believe, cut me . . . in public. . . ."

"I don't think so," answered the countess. "You see, my dear, I have already sent a note around to your uncle advising him that you are with us. I have asked him to pay me a morning call. I expect he will do so tomorrow . . . and believe me, child . . . he will not put himself at odds with my husband and myself."

"Well done, Mama!" Richard of Grey was moved to ejaculate. "That will book him!"

"Indeed," hastened Miss Avery to agree, "you are very good, and I am certain my uncle would be . . . moved to follow whatever advice you chose to direct. It is only that . . . that I feel I am imposing. I feel as though I have somehow allowed myself to become parasitic. . . . I cannot take advantage of your goodness in this manner. If you feel you could recommend me into someone's household as a governess, I would be forever in your debt. It is what I want . . . for it would make me relatively independent."

"Good gracious, girl!" cried Mary, horrified. "Independent . . . as a governess? Is that what you

119

really believe? It is no such thing. It is not for you, Dennie."

"Mary has a point there," put in Richard thoughtfully and then discovered for the hundredth time that evening her deep-blue eyes. There was a quiet loveliness in them that drew him in a way he found inexpressible, unexplainable. "And besides . . . well . . . Miss Avery, you are far too beautiful to be a governess. There is not a woman that would set you up as competition in her household."

"No . . . absolutely not. Why . . . even your own aunt was moved by that motive to forbid you her protection," put in Mary candidly.

"I find that remark annoying!" retorted Richard at once.

"I found Mrs. Clifford's action annoying," returned Mary immediately. "Hold!" interrupted Lady Grey, as it appeared as though Richard and Mary might continue heatedly in this vein for some time. "You, Richard, have made an accurate observation when you remarked that it would be difficult to place Miss Avery as a governess. She is young and beautiful and therefore generally unsuitable to the position she wishes to seek out." She turned to Denise, extended an assuaging hand. "Therefore, Denise, dear . . . I do hope you will allow yourself to be guided by me in this matter."

Miss Avery was understandably reduced to stammering acquiescence. Thus the meal progressed, perhaps a little less comfortably than it had begun, but all were in agreement on at least one matter; Miss Avery was not immediately destined to become a governess.

The gambling at White's Club was running as usual in Severn's favor. The wit was lively. His friends seemed disposed to please as they recounted humorous anecdotes and attempted to catch his attention. It was not working. More often than not he glanced across the room to the wall clock. It was nearly past ten o'clock. What was wrong with him?

Restless. Every inch of him longed to be off. Dissatisfied with what he was doing. Why? Where should he go? Lady Sefton's rout, came a voice from within his head. No, confound it, no. Mary of Montlaine would be there. He had promised himself some time away from her. His better judgment, his instinct, warned him against her company. It was dangerous!

Absurd! A chit of a girl dangerous? Preposterous. He could do very well without her dark eyes glinting, without her bubbling laughter, her unexpected quips, her outrageous manners . . . but . . . devil a bit, why should he do without her charms? He was no schoolboy to be fairly caught by such entrapments. Besides, Mary was in love with young Grey. Why shouldn't he enjoy Lady Sefton's rout? Such was his mood when he entered Lady Sefton's glittering drawing room and made his way deftly, intently, through the crush of fashionables to where Mary stood in close conversation with Richard.

*   *   *

In spite of herself Mary kept looking toward the open double doors. Where was he? Had she bored Severn this morning . . . irritated him with her hoydenish behavior? Did he regret his promise to pay her public court and make Richard jealous? Richard. She didn't need to make him jealous this evening; he was very zealous in his attentions to her. Ah, but perhaps that was so because Nina Clifford had arrived on the arm of another suitor. Did it matter any longer? What was wrong with her?

There was *something* wrong. She had felt it all evening. They had left Denise in good spirits. The mood was bantering, affectionate, flirtatious . . . yes, Richard had been flirtatious this evening, and she should have been transported to new heights, but she wasn't. Odd. Very odd . . . and then she was struck by the boyishness of his compliments, the unpolished lack of reserve . . . mannerisms she had never noticed before.

Then Severn was there, and his gray eyes found and secured her answering glance. She felt a strange skipping sensation in her chest. Her heart? What was wrong with her heart? Air. There was too much air in her throat, it was choking her. Waves of goosebumps hit her body and then were sent to perdition with a great rush of heat that set her to burning. He was taking up her hand, bending over it, engaging her dark eyes, saying her name. She was mumbling a reply. "Why . . . my lord . . . I had quite nearly given you up."

"I am flattered." he answered and led her to the dance floor.

"Are you?" She shrugged. "I don't see why you should be." He felt a rush of pique. How dare this chit? Didn't she realize he could if he wished seduce her to passion? Didn't she realize how many women had fallen under his spell . . . when he willed it?

In a measured voice just touched with hurt he said softly, "Ah, I mistake, then . . . I thought perhaps you missed me. Too puffed up in my own esteem, I imagine."

She bubbled with mirth. "Why, you are shamming me! You aren't in the least bit bothered one way or the other over anything *I* might feel."

"Now, that is where you are wrong. Just look how you have turned my love life topsy-turvy because of what you are suffering!" he returned at once.

"Why . . . whatever do you mean?"

"Have you or have you not embroiled me in your affair with Richard?"

"Well, yes, but . . ."

"But nothing, my girl. It is now common knowledge about town that the 'incomparable Montlaine' is leading Severn a pretty dance!"

She blushed hotly. "Oh . . . oh . . . my lord . . ."

He laughed. "Never mind. In truth it is believed you are but a passing fancy."

"Oh, that is a relief . . . I shouldn't like your dashing reputation ruined." Her eyes were twinkling.

He had the strongest urge to catch her up closer and taste her cherry lips so enchantingly pursed. He restrained himself. "Now, sweet Mary, what have you done with your protégée?"

"Miss Avery?" She sighed. "She wants to be a governess."

"Impossible," he returned dryly.

"Hmmm. So Richard explained to her ... but she is rather determined. Has some funny notion about putting us out. Refused to join us tonight, because she felt her uncle would be livid ... and Lady Grey agreed that it might be better to wait to take her about until she has spoken to Avery herself."

"Does she plan on speaking to him?"

"Oh, yes. Lady Grey sent him a message inviting him to call tomorrow morning. Says she will handle him right and tight."

"She never said any such thing, I'd wager." He was grinning.

"Well, no, you horrid man ... not exactly in those words ... but to that effect."

The waltz was at an end, and Richard was upon them, claiming Mary's hand. Severn's brow went up, but he bowed off gracefully and stood back to watch Richard lead Mary away from the dance floor and toward the garden doors.

"What is it, Richard? What has you suddenly so miserable?" asked Mary, for she could see he was in the throes of unhappiness.

"It is ... Nina," he breathed. "Mary ... I am nearly half-mad with rage ... with jealousy ... with disillusionment ..." They were outdoors, and he put his arm about her, for a breeze brought them a wave of cool air.

She snuggled into the crook of his arm as she had often done in the past. It was a sisterly action, unconscious on her part, accepted in the same vein by him. "What can I do, Richard?"

A pained sound escaped him. "Don't . . . don't say you told me so . . . don't point out her faults . . . oh, Mary . . . it hurts so. . . ."

"What does, Richard?"

He looked at her with a half-smile and touched her cheek. "Wise little Mary . . . yes, of course . . . *analyze*. What hurts? Losing someone who never existed . . . discovering how stupid . . . how wrong one can be about himself . . . oh, Mary . . . you look so . . . lovely . . ." He bent and dropped a light kiss upon her lips.

She did not pull away and she did not respond. This was a kiss of distraction. 'Twas not what she wanted. It was a kiss . . . quite her first real kiss . . . it was his kiss . . . Richard's kiss . . . and all she could do was stand like a stock.

Severn found himself wandering toward the garden doors. He moved outside just in time to see her neatly in Richard's arm and accepting a kiss. He stood riveted for a moment, long enough to note the kiss held no passion, long enough to experience mindless fury, long enough to know an urge to throttle young Grey . . . to pull Mary out of his embrace. Instead, he turned on his heel, found his hostess and took his leave.

Hell and fire! Fiend seize his soul for a fool!

What was this? Was he some schoolboy bent on having a schoolgirl? That was all she was, nothing more. Nothing more! What he needed was a woman . . . a beautiful woman. He made his way to a certain house on a certain street. From the curbing he could see the form of such a lovely in the window. All he need do was lay down his blunt to the madame, climb the stairs and forget Mary. . . .

Chapter Eleven

"I shall set it about that she disobeys my will . . . with your encouragement, ma'am!" seethed Mr. Avery.

Lady Grey's delicate brow went up. "Will you indeed, sir? I think not."

"And why should I not?"

"Because, Mr. Avery, your niece is of age."

"Neither my wife nor her aunt, Mrs. Clifford, sanctions this . . . this behavior. Penistone has asked for her hand . . . I have given it!"

"My dear sir, you cannot in this country force a child into marriage. Not in this day and age. It is not the thing. We may guide our children . . . we may direct them . . . but we cannot bring them willy-nilly to the altar!"

"It is for her own good. She has no living of her own . . . nothing! Who would take her in such circumstances?"

"Evidently Penistone would," returned her ladyship glibly.

"He is enchanted with her . . . it is a rare thing

. . . and he is wealthy enough to make her happy, give her a good home."

"He is not suitable, and she finds him . . . disagreeable." She sighed, for the discussion was becoming repetitive. They had been at it now some twenty minutes and there was nothing more to be said. "Resign yourself to it. We shall be taking her about with us, though she will not be brought out formally. Advise Mr. Penistone that if he wants Miss Avery's hand, he will have to wait until she has at least enjoyed something of a season."

"I shan't pay a penny of the bills she will no doubt incur," warned Avery.

"I didn't think you would, Mr. Avery." She got to her feet, went to the bellrope and when a lackey appeared nodded her dismissal. "Please show Mr. Avery the door." She bent her head. "Good day, sir."

"Now just a moment . . ." objected Avery.

The earl had just entered his home. Receiving the intelligence that Denise's uncle was in the study with Lady Grey, he immediately made his way there just in time to note that his wife was looking harassed.

"Avery?" said the earl quietly.

"Ah ... my lord, perhaps *you* will listen to reason."

"You don't possess any."

"Mad ... you are all quite mad!" ejaculated Avery.

"All the more reason for you to make haste and leave my home. There is never any saying what a madman might do . . . how violent he might get," returned the earl glaringly.

Avery bustled out of harm's way, mumbling under his breath and saying to the lackey as he left the house, "They won't get away with this. It will all come back to haunt them one day."

The earl turned to his lady. "Was it very bad, my love? You are looking a bit fagged from the encounter."

"Nonsense . . . it just touched me to think that poor lovely girl spent all those years in that dreadful man's household."

In answer to this he held up a yellow envelope and waved it before her face. "Just look what the special post brought by as I was coming in."

"Vanessa? Is it from Vanessa?"

He beamed, and she pounced upon her daughter's letter. Together they read it and then reread it, laughing over all the absurdities she had already managed to embroil herself and her husband in.

"It quite sets my knees to shaking when I think that my uncle is closeted with Lady Grey at this very moment," said Miss Avery on a hushed note.

Mary patted her arm and continued to lead her through the park at a decorous pace. "Don't fret, Dennie. Lady Grey will handle him, you may depend upon it."

Richard, who was walking just behind with his cousin Randall of Southvale, hastened to agree, "Oh, Mother is top sawyer at such things."

"I am certain you are quite right . . . but . . . it

worries me to think how he might react. . . ." Miss Avery shuddered, for she could remember vividly her uncle's behavior when he was out of humor.

Somehow Richard was beside her, taking up her arm, patting her gloved hand, "Avery may be a loose screw, but he won't dare ruffle m'mother's feathers. Why, I do believe m'father would send him flying. High stickler, m'father."

Randall took the opportunity to engage Mary in conversation. He had not been able to get her alone for some time now. Earnestly he bent to catch her dark eyes. "Mary . . . Mary . . ."

"Yes, Randy?" There was the tease ever lurking, her sense of the ridiculous ready to overset her and start her laughing.

He sensed it and bristled up immediately. "You've been avoiding me," he accused.

She arched a look at him. "Have I? If you think so, dear friend, perhaps you have an answer."

He was about to answer her in hot terms when she silenced him suddenly by taking strong hold of his upper arm. There, walking toward them, was Nina Clifford. The tall and elegant blonde had the arm of a military gentleman, and as she came closer Mary could see Richard stiffen.

"Richard . . . Richard . . ." Mary called urgently, trying to gain his attention. "Bring Dennie away . . . at once!"

Richard recalled his wits, turned a horrified expression to Miss Avery and immediately collected her up. "I am so sorry, Denise. Come . . . we can take this other avenue."

"Oh, thank you . . . for in truth I should not

like to encounter my aunt in public just yet."

They took a tree-lined path that ran along the bridle path and a moment later breathed a sigh of relief. Richard made a small jest that set them all to laughing, and it was thus that Severn, riding his dapple-gray gelding, came upon them.

Severn saw them from a distance. Something inside of him churned. His head was still heavy from the night before. What a night. He had been unable to step within madame's quarters and spend a convivial evening with one of madame's pretties. Somehow he had just been lacking in proper desire. Instead he joined a party of friends and went to Cribb's Parlor to blow a cloud and drink a few intimates under the table. This he had done, ending this morning with a head for the effort.

An appointment with his man of business took him out of the house when all he wanted to do was soak in a hot tub for hours. His mood was irritable. His hopes confused. His wants undefined. A shortcut through the park? Why not?

He hadn't expected to see Mary there, hadn't wanted to see Mary now, not this morning . . . or had he? Damn, he didn't know his own mind any longer. Had he no more will of his own? He was nearly thirty, he had known all kinds of women . . . he had always been master of his affairs, and yet, Mary scared him to death!

He could do naught. She was here among her friends . . . she was here with Richard. He pulled in his horse, tipped his hat to the ladies, nodded to the gentlemen at their side and would have moved on had not Mary in her easy, friendly manner begun cooing softly to his horse. He watched, fascinated, as the dapple gray responded to her affection.

"Ooh . . . that's a handsome boy . . . yes . . . oh, does he like to play tongue?" She spoke to the gelding as she played with his lower lip. "Handsome love . . ." Then to Severn, "My lord, he is magnificent. Is he strong in the works?"

"Rather . . . but he has won me an important wager or two." Severn smiled, for he was proud of the dapple. It was his favorite mount.

"I'll say!" agreed Richard. "Slap up to the mark, this prime 'un! Took that race to Brighton against Widdons, didn't he, Severn?"

"Yes," answered Randy, "and the other to Dover, as I recall. Bought him from Rochester, didn't you, my lord?"

"That I did. Rochester seemed to have some trouble with him . . . and no patience to school it out of him," commented Severn lightly.

"Some trouble? The man couldn't stay on him, as I recall," answered Southvale on a snort.

Mary was watching Severn throughout this. Something was wrong. There was a tightness about his mouth. There were lines under his eyes. What was it? Quietly she called his attention to herself. "You left early last night. . . ."

"You noticed? I should have thought you were too well occupied to miss me," he answered dryly.

"I always notice the departure of a friend," she answered on a surprised note.

He sighed. She was killing him. Here was this

chit, confusing him with her innocent wiles, her large devastating dark eyes. She was leaving him tongue-tied, this chit of a girl. Ludicrous, but it was so . . . and she was so beautiful in her straw bonnet and her olive-green redingote. Softly he changed the subject. "Well, Mary, does all proceed as you plan?"

She gleamed at him. "At this point, sir, the future is a mystery, but I would chance to say that it does not go against hopes, if that is what you mean."

"Hopes, Mary . . . or ambition?"

There was an intenseness in his question that startled her. She studied him. His gray eyes were troubled. She could hear the others conversing behind her. An answer was needed, but instinct warned her to be careful. What was he looking for? She thwarted him with an arched look and a question of her own.

"If there is a difference between the two, what makes the first haloed and the other grasping?"

"Because the first allows nature to take its course, and the latter is guided usually by our own hands," he answered.

"Ah, now let me consider this thing. I part from my blind friend in the hope that he may cross the crowded avenue without mishap. I go along my own path, but I have *hoped,* have I not, and therefore if he falls prey to injury it is whose fault? Lady Luck's? Nature's fault for making him blind? I am not his keeper . . . it is not my fault." She shook her head. "No, my lord, call it ambition, but I would exert myself, for it is my *ambition* that he reach safety!"

He inclined his head in some amusement. "Your sophistry is to be congratulated. However, it does not serve in the matter at hand." He stilled her with his expression. "Let it be for now, sweet Mary, for I have a pressing appointment which calls me away from further debate with you now."

She stepped aside. In spite of herself she allowed herself to ask him, and immediately chided herself after the words were out, "Perhaps, my lord, we may further discuss the subject this evening at Dreswell's soirée?"

"I think not. I am otherwise engaged," he answered softly.

"Oh." A flush heightened her color. Had she been too bold? Were her hoydenish manners putting him off? She watched him nod and take himself off from the remainder of her party. Why did she feel suddenly cold? Was there a cloud overhead? No . . . the sun still beamed. Why then had all enchantment with the fine spring day fled? And why could she summon no anticipation for the evening's entertainment?

During this time neither Severn nor Mary noticed a ravishing mort with blond hair and limpid eyes standing not very far away. Francine White gritted her teeth. Here he was again with that dark-haired chit, she thought angrily as she watched them converse. Severn seemed much taken with her, and it was said among his friends that he was paying court to a young diamond! Who was she? She must find out who his latest flirt was and just how serious the affair had become. A thought came to her and slid her mouth into a sly curve. A plan began to evolve. It needed polish, of course, and this could not be done until she had extracted some information from one or two reliable sources.

She crossed the crowded avenue and made her way to her dressmaker's. If Severn had not yet thought to close this account she would order a few more gowns made. He owed her that. Oh yes, she thought viciously, he owed her that and more . . . much more, and she meant to have it one way or another!

Chapter Twelve

Five days and nights had passed by, and Mary found herself sadly out of sorts. She pinched one dark curl over her forehead into place, smoothed over her deep red velvet gown, adjusted the pearls at her throat and ears and stepped away from the looking glass. She should have been thrilled with herself and could not understand why depression had set in and taken over her moods.

Denise Avery was enjoying her new life and rarely mentioned becoming a governess these days. Under Lady Grey's chaperonage society's minions had given her a mild welcome. She would not, of course, be any notable success, for she lacked the proper dowry, but her family name was an old and respected one and she was therefore good ton.

There too, Richard seemed to be more and more in Mary's company these days. The other night she had in fact found herself in the gardens alone with him and knew that if she had made a push for it, she would have had his kiss. Such was his mood, such was the setting, the words, but instead she had teased him, set him to bantering with her, and again they were on the level of friendship. Why? What was wrong with her?

What was so different about these last five days? Oh, to be sure, it was becoming irritating to have Randy forever at her heels ... it was of some concern to find that Lord Grey had received no less than four offers for her hand this week and that she had not even been aware that the gentlemen making these offers were seriously interested in her. It had been uncomfortable facing these young men after turning all of them down ... but that was not at the heart of her depression. Oh, to be sure, Severn had not been around. She had not seen him anywhere.

His name, however, was mentioned everywhere she went. Lud, one woman would say, Severn had done this or Severn had done that. His horses were running at Ascot and sure to pay, the men would say. His last speech in the House of Lords had been brilliant. And then his name was coupled with Francine White's, and Mary felt an odd permeating rush of wild emotion she could not define.

They had been at Vauxhall the other evening. Francine was on stage in a gown that scarcely hid her lovely flesh, and Mary had remarked to Denise that she thought the woman a stunning beauty.

"Oh yes," agreed Denise. "But I cannot like her style ... and, Mary, her voice is lacking in quality."

To this Richard leaned into his cousin Randall and remarked jestingly, "Lord Randy . . . be glad you didn't take that bird under your wing. I hear she has cost Severn a pretty sum."

Randall had frowned at him and informed him haughtily, "My interests are elsewhere."

Mary had gone rigid. She stared at the beautiful woman on stage and felt something twist in her stomach. This was absurd. Men did these things. Men took ladies of that sort under their protection. Especially men like Severn. Why, her own brother had, she was sure, often indulged this weakness. Severn and Francine White. Severn and Francine White. It came harshly, repeatedly. Stop!

This was nonsense. Who was Severn to her? Naught. But . . . he had said such things. In playacting . . . at her request. Severn was nothing to her. Nothing . . . and still she looked for him everywhere she went.

A maid appeared at her door and advised her apologetically that she was awaited in the central hall.

"Oh dear . . . I am so sorry," Mary cried and picked up her black velvet cloak.

She was hailed as she reached the stairs,

"Mary! There you are. Come on, we want to get there on time, for there is bound to be a squeeze at the door," admonished Richard.

She smiled at Denise and said breathlessly that she had been daydreaming as Richard ushered them outdoors to his waiting carriage.

*　　*　　*

Severn ran his fingers through his russet-colored hair. He had been out of town on business these last five days. It had not been a thing he couldn't have put off, but he had thought it prudent to leave London and Mary for a time. Get his senses back in order. Remind himself what being tied to a woman could mean. He kept himself well occupied with his affairs. He should have stayed away another week, but in a sudden frenzy he broke down and hastened to town.

An afternoon at the club left him itching to find her, but he restrained himself and accepted an invitation to form one of Petersham's party for the theater. Lady Jersey quipped incessantly in his ear, Petersham went on and on about a new snuffbox he had just discovered, and relief came only when he found Tom Moore coming toward him.

"Tom, you old dog! It's been an age! Scribbling, as always?" cried Severn, pleased to find the poet looking well.

"Aye, about love of Ireland . . . damn if I don't return there soon."

Severn sighed. "Hmm. Things must seem different for you now what with Byron gone. What do you hear from him these days and is it true that Claire Clairmont bears him a child?"

"It is true, and he is in Venice seducing all the women and falling in love with but one."

He was obliged to laugh over this and some other news Tom chose to impart to him until suddenly he seemed to be in a vacant room, vacant but for one being. She sat, her shoulders small, delicate and white in a blaze of red velvet. A red feather tickled her ear. Dark curls clustered about her face. Severn felt his heart spring up from its depths, and his gray eyes were held by an invisible force emanating from a pair of dark eyes across the theater galley. Absently and to the poet's surprise he excused himself and found that his legs carried him with a will of their own.

Mary saw him. He was standing in pleasant conversation with Tom Moore. He was laughing. He was happy. There was no sign that he had missed her, that he was looking for her presence here. Only she looked! Oh, it was a lowering thought. His gray eyes discovered her . . . he was coming her way.

Indignation flooded her heart. Why? No answer. How dare he just wander over and expect a welcome? Friends did not disappear and reappear without explanation . . . without warning. He was . . . he was . . . unforgivable. Nonsense. He owed her nothing. She looked around for Denise and Richard and remarked to Randall that she thought the play would start soon, and then Severn was here.

"Mary?" It was almost a whisper.

She turned and found him nodding his greeting to Randall. She allowed him a frosty smile. "Ah, Severn. How nice. It would appear that we have quite a full house here tonight."

"Well, it isn't often that Kean stays sober long enough to gift us with a performance of *Hamlet*. He is superb in the part," answered Severn quietly.

Their attention was momentarily diverted from

each other by a loquacious young man in the pit below. Randall studied the boisterous individual a moment before releasing a gleeful exclamation that it was indeed Smitty.

"Capital! Lord, but I haven't seen Smitty since he put a bear in . . ." He recollected himself and caught the sentence in time. "Do excuse me just a moment, Mary . . . I will return directly."

Mary was about to protest when something, she knew not what, stopped her. She watched him leave, waved demurely at Lady Jersey across the room. Paid intent attention to the passing fashionables and totally avoided Severn's eye.

He frowned. "What is it, Mary?"

"What is what?"

"Don't tease me, Mary, it is not your way."

"Is it not? How can you be sure? You say I am not a tease . . . but then I remember your saying to me . . . *some days ago* . . . that I was ambitious." She could have kicked herself as soon as this was out. She hadn't wanted to refer to his absence.

"I have been away on business, you know," he advised her quietly, hating himself for giving in to her already. Here she was demanding in her way to be given an explanation for his disappearance. What right had she? None . . . yet he found himself complying, he found himself accounting to her.

"Oh?" It did not altogether mollify her. "I am certain your efforts met with success. I hear everything you undertake is always brilliantly executed."

He frowned. What was this? Why was she

baiting him? Why was she bristling? Better to herd the subject elsewhere. "And you, Mary? What have you been at?"

"We have been jauntering about. Putting Nina Clifford's nose out of whack with Denise ... visiting Vauxhall ... where we saw Francine White perform the other night." Again she could have screamed with vexation at her lack of restraint. She hadn't meant to mention Francine White.

His gray eyes flickered, but he ignored the provocative remark.

"And what of Richard?"

"He no longer mopes after Nina Clifford, if that is what you mean. It is surprising, really, for she has, I understand, cast out her lures to him again. However, Randy says that her recent behavior gave Richard a disgust of her."

"So, he is yours for the taking?" There was an undercurrent beneath the lightness of his question.

She sighed. "I suppose he was ... I don't know. A few nights back I suppose I could have made the attempt ... I suppose I could have caught him on the rebound."

"Then why, sweet Mary ... why didn't you?"

"Oh I don't know ... the impulse was gone."

"Then who will it be? Randall?"

She looked at Severn strangely for a long moment and kept her answer to herself, for the earl and his lady had arrived from their dinner engagement and were closely followed by Richard, Randall and Denise. Severn excused himself after passing the amenities and Mary saw no more of him that night.

Morning came and found Denise Avery sitting alone in the drawing room with an envelope in her trembling fingers. Some days ago she had applied to an advertisement in the *Times*. Here already was the response.

It would be the end of a dream. The last week had been a glorious dream, and Richard had been a prince. He was everything she had ever wanted in a man. He was kind, good and so very handsome. He was attentive, gentle, witty . . . and in love with her aunt!

Mary said no. She said Richard was cooling toward Nina Clifford, but she wasn't so sure. It was difficult to know just what Richard felt these days . . . and then there was Mary. Did Mary want Richard for herself? Early in their relationship, in their first meeting, Denise had suspected this . . . but was it still true? Mary, her own dear friend, her savior. If Richard were free from Nina's charms, would he go to Mary? Yes, he must if that is what Mary wanted.

She tore open the envelope with the letter opener and spread out the ivory paper in her lap.

Dear Miss Avery:
Your family name is known to us, which to some extent excuses your lack of references. If you will make yourself available within the following week for an interview, we should be happy to consider you for the post of com-

panion to the dowager Lady Augusta Holland, who was for many years your mother's friend.

Very truly yours,
Lady Sarah Holland
Farnbourgh

She read the letter twice over and sighed. It was an answer to her problem. It was a prospect for the future. She would keep quiet about it, make up her mind about it, and if she went, she knew she would have to do so quickly, before she lost the courage to depart.

Mary's dark short curls were studded with pearl egrets. At her throat was a black ribbon embellished with a pearl cluster. Over her alluring body she wore a high-waisted white gown whose sheer long sleeves and flounced hem were embroidered with black velvet fern leaves. She looked stunning as she entered Lady Dorchester's ballroom beside Lady Grey.

Richard escorted Denise, who looked much in spirits in the pale-green silk gown she wore. They made quite an entrance, thought Lady Grey proudly.

Mary was restless. She scanned the room hopefully, but he was not there, and she knew a surging disappointment.

"Well timed," came Severn's deep voice at her back.

Relief swept her body, and she felt idiotic. He was here. He had come. She arched herself invitingly. "High praise indeed, but is it, my lord, to yourself or to me?" The tease was in her eyes.

"To myself, sweetness. A moment spent here without you would have been insipid sport. A moment later might have found you already partnered, and I have this ludicrous desire to be the first to waltz you on the floor tonight." With this he led her out.

He was so very near. He held her so very tightly. She was aware of him, far too aware of him, and it brought the blush to her cheeks. He threw back his head and laughed. "Mary ... what *are* you thinking?"

"Why?"

"You are blushing furiously, and in all the times I've been with you, this is the first you have put on a missish air!"

She giggled at that and glanced up at his gray laughing eyes.

"It is because I was thinking that you are very ... virile."

He chortled. "Why, Mary ... a compliment ... from you?"

"Am I so backward with them?"

"Yes." He was in a jovial mood.

"Well, my lord, 'tis because you have not often given me reason to issue them."

"But tonight I have?" He was teasing her outrageously.

She almost regretted her little burst of honesty. "You look well in black, my lord. It sets off your russet hair ... your broad shoulders. But hold ... these are things you must hear from

ountless damsels." Her eyes were glinting.
"Quite right, but never has it meant so much
o me before," he answered glibly.

"Wretch!" she returned.

Nina Clifford had been making mistakes one
after another. Even so, had she made any real
concerted effort to recall Richard of Grey to her
side, he would have been there. Instead, she chose
o show him just how many men were willing to
replace him. This served only to buck up his
pride. She chose to write missives chatising him
and Lady Grey for housing and promoting her
niece when it was against Avery's will. This served
o put him on the defensive. She chose to cut her
niece in society. This served to set him up as
Denise's knight, to shoulder her against her aunt,
and it therefore put Nina Clifford in the worst of
ights. Even so, had she not brought Felix Penistone with her to the Dorchester ball, she still
might have made a recovery with Richard.

Randall watched Severn swish Mary out of reach
and in some consternation he turned to Denise.
"Waltz, Dennie?"

She smiled and took his arm, but before they
had taken a step a voice called them around and
Denise was facing her aunt and Felix Penistone.
She went white and felt her knees weaken.
Randall patted her hand.

"Denise . . . here is Mr. Penistone wanting a
few moments' conversation with you."

"Denise . . . how good . . . how very good it is to
see you," said Penistone in his low voice.

Denise stammered a blushing greeting. Randall frowned and said, "Look here . . . we were just about . . ."

"Surely, Randall, you would not begrudge me a few moments of my niece's time?" said Nina sweetly.

"Perhaps Denise is too forgiving to do so, perhaps my cousin here is too polite to do so, but I assure you, madam, I have no qualms in the matter!" said Richard, suddenly appearing. He turned to his cousin. "Lead Denise out, will you old boy?" He watched them take the floor.

Nina Clifford was wild with rage. "How dare you! You have insulted poor Mr. Penistone here."

"Have I?" Richard of Grey smiled.

"Mrs. Clifford . . . it is obvious to me that my suit is totally unwelcome. Under the circumstances, I must withdraw it," said Penistone gravely.

"Mr. Penistone . . . do but reconsider . . ."

"I shall be happy to whenever Miss Avery comes to her senses."

"Penistone, Miss Avery has all her senses about her, make no mistake, and if I find you annoying her in the future, I shall gladly draw your cork!" offered Richard sweetly.

Penistone huffed and turned away. Nina Clifford turned on Richard.

"Did you intend such rudeness? Is it your wish to alienate my affections, Richard?"

"Have you, Nina, ever once considered my part in this? Have you ever considered Denise's feelings? Did I . . . Nina, did I ever know you?"

"You miserable . . . but what else could I expect from a *boy?*" With this she was off.

As Severn waltzed Mary around the floor more than a few heads turned to watch them. More than a few whispers went around the room. When had Severn ever lasted so long with such a miss? Never! She was not in his usual style . . . to be sure, a beauty, but not in his fashion. She was not quite a woman . . . far too lively . . . far too green. More than one of Severn's intimates raised his brows in wonder.

Lady Grey took her son's arm. "Richard . . . Severn seems as taken with Mary now as he was before he went away."

Before Richard could answer this, his father appeared and added, "More so, I think, my love."

She turned to her husband. "Mary will be hurt in this . . . ?"

"It is a possibility," said the earl thoughtfully.

"Not while I am around it isn't!" retorted Richard, much in the mood for battle. He stalked off in Mary's direction, for the waltz was nearly at an end.

Severn bowed over Mary's hand and allowed Richard to take her off. "What are you doing, Richard?" Mary inquired after a moment.

"Randy wants a dance with you," he answered curtly.

"Well, all right . . . but he could have . . ."

"Won't have you making a gapeseed over that libertine, Mary, and so I warn you!"

She stopped and pulled out of his touch. "Rich-ard?" she said sweetly.

"Yes?"

"Go to the devil," she answered just as sweetly and would have loped off had he not caught her hand.

"Come on . . . I want to talk with you."

She pulled out of his grip. "No."

Randy appeared. "Mary . . . ?"

"I would love to, Randy." With which she went off for yet another waltz. This had not progressed very far when Severn set every tongue to wag-ging by doing the remarkable. He cut in on Randall of Southvale for his second consecutive waltz with Mary of Montlaine!

"This is not the thing," whispered Mary as he twirled her about.

"No, it is not, and both Richard and Randall look as though they should like to have my head . . . but Lady Grey very wisely has directed Richard to dance with Miss Avery and has sent Randall off for lemonade, I imagine." He was leading her toward the garden doors, spinning her around, adroitly setting her in place. "Miss Montlaine . . . you are looking a bit flushed. Shall we quit the waltz and take a short walk in the garden?"

She should refuse. The waltz had not ended. He was doing this because he knew they would not be missed until the end of the dance. She should not go with him. She put her hand on his arm and allowed him to lead her outside.

He looked at her for a long moment. "Young

Grey is jealous, Mary. I think your game is fairly won."

"Stop it! Don't make it sound so calculating, and besides . . . I don't know if my 'game,' as you put it, is the same as it was a few weeks ago." She was incurably honest.

"Ah, is it Randall, then?" His eyes were intent on her own. "Just what are you holding out for?"

" 'Tis simple, my lord, and you are answered in one word: *love*."

He had her soundly in his arms. There was no holding himself back any more. A guttural release, scarcely audible: "Damn!"

She discovered his grip was binding and tantalizing. She was responding to a kiss fiery with passion, and then she felt herself flung away.

"Love? Are you holding out for love right now, Mary? Or are you like the rest of your kind?"

She hauled off and gave his face a resounding slap. A moment later she was gone, and he stood in the gardens wondering how he had come to this pass. He hadn't meant to kiss her? Yes he had. He hadn't meant to insult her? Yes he had. Why? What was it she was doing to him?

Chapter Thirteen

Francine White played idly with the material Madame Burton laid out before her. She scarcely gave it notice, for she was not there to buy a gown.

A few coins placed in the right sewing girl's hand some days ago had won her the information that Miss Montlaine was due in this morning for a gown fitting.

Mary of Montlaine. It was being said by Severn's intimates that he had finally had his heart neatly twanged. Would he come up to scratch? The clubs were reverberating with the question. Odds were being taken. It was humiliating. How could she bear it, Severn stolen from her by a chit of a girl?

Well, there were several avenues open to her, but first she would make the girl suffer. If Miss Montlaine's heart was in this, Francine knew a sure way to prick it ... if not her heart, her pride. Either way, this morning would serve, and as it happened she had not long to wait.

Lady Grey descended the steps of her carriage

and turned to eye Mary. Something was bothering her charge, but she could not tell what. Something that had occurred last night. It was all very odd, and Mary was not confiding her trouble.

"Mary . . . why don't you go ahead to Madame Burton's? I shall be there in a moment, as I should like to stop at my jeweler's for a moment and see if he can repair my brooch while I wait."

Mary nodded and picked up the skirts of her stylish blue silk redingote. She was greatly troubled by her last encounter with Severn. Everything about it gnawed at her brain, at her heart. Why had she kissed him? Oh, he took you by surprise, she answered. *Liar,* still another voice called. *You wanted that kiss!*

What then if that is true? Am I immoral? *Stupid* . . . one kiss doesn't make you a jade. But I wanted to kiss him . . . I wanted his touch . . . and what is more . . . I wanted so very different words from him from the ones he flung at me!

She entered the shop, and Madame Burton immediately began to bustle over her, ushering her to a seat, placing a fashion magazine in her lap and disappearing with the advice that she would return directly with Miss Montlaine's gown.

Francine moved and caught Mary's eye. Mary's delicate dark brow went up, and she returned Francine's stare. Should she compliment the woman on her singing capabilites? It would be the nice thing to do. "Miss White, is it not?" Mary smiled.

"Ah, so I do know you. I thought so," answered Francine, going over to her immediately.

"No, I don't think so, but I have had the pleasure of hearing you sing at Vauxhall," answered Mary amiably.

"Vauxhall . . ." The woman sighed. "It will be a long time before I am able to sing there again."

"Oh? I am sorry to hear that," answered Mary politely.

Francine White frowned. This remark had been intended to urge Mary on to ask why. She hesitated and said in a low voice, "I am here to have a dress altered, for soon I shall grow out of my gowns."

Mary was amused. "Really? Are you planning on eating a great deal?" It was a tease.

"Lud, yes. They say that one must do so when with child." She lowered her lashes effectively; the lie flowed freely, devastatingly, from her lips.

Mary stiffened. Here was Severn's mistress, and she was saying that she was with child. "You . . . you are very slim still . . . I would imagine it will be some length of time before you need your gowns altered."

"La, but I hope so . . . however, as this gown is Severn's favorite, I thought I should have it ready. . . ." A girl came bearing a gown of silver sarsenet over silver satin. "Here it is," she said to Mary. "Well . . . go on, child, wrap it up and I shall be on my way." Again she turned to Mary. "It has been so nice chatting with you."

Mary smiled and nodded when a moment later

Francine was leaving with her package. She showed no sign to Francine White that her news had disturbed her, but she waited till the woman was out of sight before she got to her feet and called to Madame Burton.

"Please . . . madame . . . Lady Grey will come here . . . tell her I was feeling unwell and took a hackney home. . . ." With this she rushed out of the store.

A hack was hailed and told her direction, and she sat back and held herself in check. What did it matter? Francine White was bearing his child. His child . . . Francine White. What did it matter? It happened all the time . . . it was the way of her world . . . and who was Severn to her? But why . . . why did he kiss her . . . and confuse her mind?

Once at home and safely secured in her room, she released her bottled emotions and cried soundly into her pillow. A knock filtered through her sobs, and she caught herself up, sniffed and called out shakily.

"Yes? Who is it?"

"It's Denise. Mary, are you quite all right? May I come in?"

"I . . . I am tired, Dennie . . . that is all. . . . I shall see you later."

"But Richard is here, Mary . . . he would like to take us out for a ride in Hyde Park. Do come."

Mary put her hand to her head. It was throbbing; she couldn't bear it. What did she care for a ride in the park? "No . . . you go with him, Dennie . . . please. I really do need a nap."

"Mary? I . . . can I help?"

"Go on, Denise . . . please." She was losing patience. She wanted to be alone. She wanted to sort things out in her head.

Denise turned away from the closed door. What was this? Had she heard Mary crying? What was wrong with Mary?

It was a question that went around the dinner table in the Greys' household that evening. What was wrong with Mary? Lady Grey had come in hurriedly from Madame Burton's and had gone immediately to Mary's room. Mary had not admitted her but had reiterated what she had told Denise. She was fatigued, needed only a nap, some quiet . . . a period of privacy.

It was not like Mary. Something was wrong, and it had started last night at the Dorchester ball. To be sure, Mary's spirits were not lively this morning . . . but this . . . this was quite more serious, for Mary had not come down to dinner and had not touched the dinner tray sent up to her room.

The Greys and Denise parted from her doubtfully that evening. They presented conjectures to one another as their carriage brought them nearer to Almack's.

"Perhaps the child has contracted a fever? Should we not call in a doctor?" This from the earl, who sat pensively gazing at his wife's drawn features.

Richard moved beside his father. "Said something last night about feeling poorly . . . yes . . . she did seemed a bit flushed."

157

"I don't think Mary is ill . . . at least not in the way you mean," said her ladyship quietly.

Denise looked stricken. Was Mary suffering a bout of heartache? Was it because of Richard? She had sensed from the start that Mary might be interested in Richard . . . and yet she had allowed herself to respond to his overtures. Even knowing that Mary cared for him she allowed herself to become attached to him. She was a viper to so serve Mary. She would put a stop to this growing feeling between herself and Richard. She must. She turned her face away and gazed out the window.

"What do you mean, Mama?" asked Richard with a frown. "About Mary being ill but not ill?"

"I think our Mary is suffering a heartache," said the countess sadly.

"Severn!" exploded Richard. "I shall have his head. Do you think he offered her a slight?"

"Nonsense!" ejaculated the earl. "Severn is a gentleman, and any fool who has looked their way could see he was greatly taken with Mary. He has not brought her low."

"Then why is she suffering a decline?" demanded Richard pugnaciously.

"We don't know that she is. Good Lord . . . the girl has said she is fatigued. Shall we allow it to be so or jump to ridiculous suspicions?" answered his father.

This was not answered, and each of the earl's party drew on his own knowledge of Mary and came up with entirely different conclusions. However, only Lady Grey came closest to the truth, and when Severn approached her in Almack's assembly rooms, she did not smile.

He bent over her gloved hand. "Lady Grey . . . elegant as ever. . . ." He hesitated, feeling very much like a schoolboy. "I haven't seen Mary about this evening."

"Oh? Have you been looking?" returned Lady Grey unemotionally and still without a smile.

A frown descended lightly over his gray eyes, and he answered in a grave tone, hoping she would understand, "It is my object always these days to seek out Mary."

She allowed one brow to answer him before saying softly, "Our Mary is home tonight. She was a bit fatigued and declined to join us."

He felt an anxious sensation course swiftly through his veins. He was master no more of his own emotions. He restrained himself. "I am sorry to hear it. Please convey my best wishes to her. I trust she will be feeling more the thing by the morrow."

Lady Grey inclined her head, and her eyes dismissed him. He allowed it, but then stood a moment before moving away. What was wrong here? Was Mary really only recuperating from too many balls, too many excursions? No, he rather thought not. She didn't look a bit tired last evening. Last evening? He could remember vividly the feel of her in his arms, the touching of lips and the shocked hurt when he had spat out his venom at her. Fury followed hurt. How beautiful she had looked when she collected the insult and sent it back across his face.

He had been a raging devil then. He had not sought her out and he had not apologized. Briskly and without looking her way he had left the ball. He had gone home to his fire and his thoughts. His thoughts? Mary. She was a girl ... to be sure, a sprightly lovely girl ... but he had had so many wondrously beautiful women in his time. He felt as though he were suddenly starting life over, for no other emotion was like to this. No other woman had brought him to this pass, and it scared him into stupidity.

Raw fear. That was what he was experiencing. Mary scared him into clumsiness, and suddenly he had behaved the cad. He didn't know what to do with her, how to win her, how to gain control. He—the lover, the seducer, the conquerer of women—was reduced to the antics of a jealous boy.

Almack's had no more lure for him. He had come only for Mary. He was soon taking leave of Lady Jersey. Lady Grey watched him go. It was a puzzlement, for he had an unmistakable look about him. His inquiry about Mary had been pointed ... why, he had almost made a declaration. A man like Severn did not drop such a remark without purpose. He had said it was his purpose always to seek Mary out. He had departed as soon as he had ascertained that Mary was not present. What was this? Had Severn been ensnared by Mary? If this was so, then her suspicions about Mary's nurturing a broken heart were unfounded. But Mary was at home. . . .

She sighed over the problem and noticed her

son twirling Denise Avery on the floor. Here now was another unexpected development. To be sure, Denise was lovely in her way, but not in Richard's style, and certainly she was not as vivaciously beautiful as Mary. Yet, Richard had forgotten about his attachment to Nina Clifford. That had been relegated to his youth and he was emerging a man, but not for Mary.

Another sigh escaped her. How very contrary was all this to her expectations. Denise was soft-spoken and reticent. Although she would smile sweetly upon his antics, upon Mary's jests and lively banter, she never really participated. Her tastes in colors and clothes were far too simple, and while not dowdy they did her no credit. Yet, more and more did Richard smile her way, and there was something in the smile that his mother had never seen in him before.

She was taken away from her musings by Lady Jersey, who demanded she attend her gossip. She listened to the latest *on dit* and was presently diverted enough to forget what roads her children were exploring.

Lord Severn found himself directing his driver to take him home. He was in no mood for the club or his friends. Mary's absence this night proved a severe blow to his plans. He had meant to seek her out and level himself for her. He had behaved the scoundrel, and so he meant to admit. She was not present, and he could not believe his Mary was suffering from fatigue. No, she had been hurt by him.

He paced for a time. He attempted to read. He donned his cloak and went for a walk. He stopped by Cribb's Parlor and chatted for a time with friends but found he could not concentrate on what was being addressed to him. He returned home and attempted sleep. He tossed, he turned, and suddenly knew what he wanted to do.

He lit a branch of candles and sat at his writing desk. There he sat composing, ripping to shreds, composing, reading, ripping to shreds, until he had at last put down something near to what he wanted her to read.

Mary, sweet Mary,

It was with bitter disappointment that I did not find you at Almack's last night. There was so much I wanted to say. I was told that you were suffering a bout of fatigue and hope that this letter finds you fully recovered.

You and I know what apology is due you, but in its stead I would take a few lines from Cowper and fit them to my purpose;

Thy chestnut locks, always bright,
Are more lovely in my sight
Than golden beams of orient light,
My Mary!

For could I view nor them nor thee,
What sight worth seeing could I see?
The sun would rise in vain for me,
My Mary!

I humbly beg that you will grant me an interview this morning. My servant shall await your response.

> Believe me your very obedient,
>
> Severn

His letter was delivered to Mary early that morning, and she sat in bed trembling as she read it through. Several reactions might have been expected. Another girl might have been flustered into confusion. Another girl might have been moved to doubt. Surely any girl would have been flattered, but Mary was only furious!

Here he was quoting—misquoting—Cowper . . . intimating that he was romantically attached to her . . . that he had formed a *tendre* in her direction . . . when he was the father of another woman's child! Fiend seize his rakish soul and send it to perdition. He had himself a mistress whom he clothed and apparently cared for, yet here he was making signs to her. How dare he!

She went to her own writing desk and rigorously set out to scribble him into oblivion.

Severn,

I take leave to inform you that your epistle confirms my newly found belief that you are an unprincipled rogue. You are a profligate and a cad. You despise women and treat them accordingly.

I shall not grant you an interview, and if you dare to approach me when next we chance

163

to cross one another's paths, I shall be pleased
to cut you dead!

Mary of Montlaine

She sent this note off before she had time to
further consider. She had put him soundly in his
place. She had set him away from her world. No
more would she find his gray eyes twinkling at
her. No more would his lips curve suddenly into
that engaging smile he had shared with her. No
more would she warm to his many charming
mannerisms or hear his deep voice teasing in her
ear. It was what she wanted, never to see him
again. Therefore, she naturally burst into tears!

Chapter Fourteen

Mary wrapped her shawl about her shoulders and moved to her bedroom window. From there she had a view of the street below, and her delicate brow went up in some surprise as she saw Denise hurriedly cross the street. She wore one of Vanessa's cloaks which had been altered for her. In her hand she swung a bandbox. There was something about the set of her features that was disturbing.

Mary rang her bell rope. A moment later her maid appeared and bobbed a curtsy. Mary smiled at her.

"Cecie . . . did you help Miss Avery dress this morning?"

The young girl looked a little flustered. "No . . . no, miss . . . I did not."

"Cecie . . . you know something. What is it? Where has Miss Avery gone?"

"I wouldn't be knowing that . . . but . . . oh, miss . . . she asked me not to say a word until she had been gone at least an hour. . . ."

"Cecie! What is it? Where has she gone?" This with alarm as Mary came forward.

"Well . . . I happened in on Miss Avery . . . as she was folding a dress into a bandbox. She . . . she told me . . . there was a letter for you on her mantel shelf and I was to give it to you one hour after she left the house. Said . . . said it was important that I obeyed. . . ."

Mary did not wait for more. She ran past the maid, across the hall and into the bright-yellow room Denise had been using. On the mantel shelf was the sealed envelope. Mary tore it open at once.

Dear Mary,

Forgive me. I know now that you are pushing Richard in my way because you think I love him. It is just like you to sacrifice, but my dearest friend, I shall not allow it.

Do not worry about me. I have a post waiting for me at my intended destination. When I am settled I shall write to you. Please thank Lord and Lady Grey for all their kindnesses. There is nothing I can do to repay them but to leave.

With much affection always,
Denise Avery

P.S. I have taken only one of the gowns Lady Grey was so generous as to have altered for me, and only the poorest of the cloaks. Please, please forgive me.

Mary went into action. Systematically she began

opening Denise's bureau drawers until she came across the advertisement Denise had answered. A companion? Denise was running away to become a companion to the dowager at Farnbourgh. Insufferable . . . and why? Sacrifice? What did she mean? And then it came to her. Denise thought she was pining over Richard. Denise was in love with Richard!

There was only one course of action that could be taken. She threw off her shawl, ran back to her own room, hastily donned her redingote and bonnet and took the stairs. Tootles came forward and braved a question.

"Shall we expect you to luncheon, miss?" In this manner he was serving his lady, for she would most certainly wish to know what Mary was about running out of the house in this fashion.

She allowed him a quick, "No . . . and please tell Lady Grey not to worry . . . I am only off to fetch Richard and Denise!"

Francine White paced in her bedroom. She twisted her fingers and her pale eyes were frosty with her thoughts. Tom Lewis stretched as he watched her. His eyes wandered over her body. She looked, as ever, ravishing in her black lace lingerie. How could he bear life without her? But he had to or she would kill him in the end!

More and more she was obsessed with avarice. Her present plan to gain financial independence frightened him. He had agreed to do her bidding. Why? Because he could not refuse her a thing . . .

but after this, if she did not keep her promise and set up house as his wife, he would leave her. He could share her no more. No more. How it had hurt to know that Severn had been with her . . . Severn . . . all those others . . . but no more. She had promised him. In return for this deed, she would go away with him.

"You must be careful, Tom . . . you must wait for the right moment," she warned him.

"Never fear, love. I knows how the thing must be done. Mind, I ain't saying I approve of this piece of bobbery."

She studied him a long moment. "Tom . . . you are not backing out?"

He threw off a smile and shrugged. "It's a queer fetch, Francie m'darling, as more or less I've been pound dealing all m'life . . . but I gave ye m'word . . . for yers."

"Pound dealing?" She laughed, went to his knee and took up position there. She stroked his head. "Was it pound dealing when you were free-trading in Cornwall?"

"That's respectable, that is! Prigging off some quality chit ain't!"

"She won't be hurt. What's the harm?"

He sighed. "None, if your plan goes off well enough, but there's places that don't fit."

"Such as?"

"Jest how are we to get the ready delivered? Where is he to leave it, and how will I know he won't have a beadle or two laying in wait?"

" 'Tis simple enough. He will be informed to take the money himself on horseback and ride

ιe Charing Cross Road. He is to ride the road
ntil he is told to stop and chuck the satchel.
√hen we have inspected the contents and when
'e are free and clear we will release Miss Mont-
ιine."

"What if he don't go for it? Could be yer wrong
bout him and this chit."

"I am not wrong, and if he does not lay out his
wn blunt, well, then the Greys or Montlaines
'ill ... but *he*, Severn, is to deliver it! I want
im humiliated ... defeated ... and this is my
'ay."

He studied her a long moment. "Right, then ...
ll have to watch her comings and goings, for I
ιean for us to snabble her without a fight."

"I trust you to handle it, Tom." She was in his
rms. "Then we will go away ... we'll invest in a
ιill in the north and settle down ... forget about
ondon ... about Vauxhall ... eh, Tom?"

He wasn't sure she meant it. There was never
ny being sure with Francine, but he had his
opes, so he agreed and kissed her sweetly.

It was just about that moment that some dis-
ance away in Duke Street Lord Severn sat read-
ιg and rereading Mary's answer to his letter.

A frown set his countenance sternly. She called
im a cad. Yes, he had behaved the cad. Freely
e admitted it to his four walls. He should not
ave so brutally kissed her. Unprincipled rogue?
Jow really that was coming it a bit strong! Un-
rincipled rogue indeed. No one had ever said
hat of him before.

169

She called him a profligate . . . she accused him of despising women and treating them accordingly. This too he found shocking. He was no such thing. True, he had had his share of women . . . he was no monk . . . but neither was he a profligate. Despise women? Not so . . . he had never mistreated a woman. Always he had been honest with his bits of muslin. Never had he tampered with a virgin . . . never before, that is. What was this? Well, perhaps he held her sex not in the highest esteem, but surely he had never given her reason to suspect him of ill-treating women.

Not grant him an interview? He had half expected this. He was already beginning to know Mary, understand her design of thought. She was evidently still annoyed with him for his cavalier behavior, and she had that right, of course. Cut him? He smiled to himself. Yes, he imagined that she would coldly turn away . . . but he would not allow it.

Very well, he would give her a few days to cool down. It would not be easy, for every fiber of his heart and mind yearned to be with her, to see her, talk to her, make her understand. However, he had brought himself to this pass, and there was nothing for it now but to turn the tables around and handle it and her properly this time. He was neither daunted nor devastated by her sharp epistle. It was important now to keep himself busy, and it was with this intent that he took himself off to Manton's for some shooting practice. Time and patience, that was all he needed to wheedle himself back into Mary's good graces.

And then, Severn? What then? he asked himself. Fear kept his head from recognizing, translating, the answer his heart immediately gave forth.

Mary shot past Richard's stiff butler and demanded the man produce his employer. The austere retainer seemed inclined to refuse this; however, Richard appeared in time to save the moment and the man from severe attack.

"Mary!" Clearly he was shocked. It was not at all the thing for a maid to arrive at bachelor lodgings unescorted.

"I know, I know, I am disreputable, but if you will gather up your hat and gloves we can be off, for there is no time. She must already be at the stage and on her way to Farnbourgh."

Randall had been reposing with a cup of coffee in Richard's small study. The sound of Mary's voice brought him into the hall.

"Mary!" he repeated, much in his cousin's style.

"Oh, you here, Randy? How convenient. Well, then . . . come on, get your things. My hack is waiting outside."

"Well, at least she had the good sense to come in a hack," said Randy as he made to obey.

"What the deuce is the difference what she came in?" snapped Richard. "She shouldn't be here, and well you know it."

"No, she shouldn't, but just think what the tattlemongers would say if her carriage stood outdoors!"

"Eh . . . yes, that's true. With any good luck no one saw her enter, and perhaps between us we can fend off notice her way when we depart."

"What is all this to anything?" demanded Mary on a note of exasperation. "Didn't you hear me, Richard? Denise has run off to Farnbourgh!"

"What?" ejaculated Richard of Grey. "Is that what you are here about? Good God! Come on, then. . . ."

Randall followed, shaking his head. "I say! What would she want to go there for? Devilish place, Farnbourgh. Not in the mode, you know. . . ."

Denise purchased her stage ticket with the money she had obtained by selling the one piece of jewelry she had owned. It was a small gold heart, and it had been her mother's. Never before had she been without it. She took up her seat next to a heavy-set woman who smiled at her and began chattering away about her recent visit to London.

A clerk joined them, curtly advising them that he felt the stage was overloaded with baggage and he hoped they would not be squeezed. This hope was blown to bits when a middle-aged woman of substantial proportions and her three children entered the coach.

Denise chose to look out the window and daydream. Very soon the stage would start rumbling toward Farnbourgh and her new life. She would never see Richard of Grey again, but that was as it should be, for no doubt he would marry Mary. It was a dull ache, and she attempted to brush it aside.

The driver was drinking off his bumper of ale, taking his leave of friends, nodding to his passengers as he went past the coach door. He was climbing up, taking the reins, releasing the brake. Everything was over. Her dream was shattered.

"Stop!" shouted a feminine and yet very authoritative voice. The coach wheels screeched, and the driver looked around with a frown.

"Lookee 'ere . . . we be full up . . ."

Richard was out of the hack, he was pulling open the stagecoach door, taking Denise's arm. "Out, you silly goose!"

"Eh . . . what's this?" objected the stout woman with the three children. "Leave the girl alone, you . . . you . . ."

"Oh no, please . . . he is a friend," cried Denise.

"A friend, is it?" objected the clerk. "Well, this is no social function. He is detaining us all."

"Come on then, Dennie . . . out with you," cried Richard jovially. "We are holding all these people back!"

"But . . . but Richard, you do not understand . . ."

"Perhaps he does not," said Mary, joining them, "but I assure you, my friend, that I do. Come, Denise . . . you really should be ashamed of yourself, holding all these fine people up." There was a tease in her eyes.

Denise blushed hotly. "Please, Mary . . ."

"Don't want to go to Farnbourgh," added Randy, bringing up the rear. "Dashed if it ain't a queer place to go to."

"What is wrong with Farnbourgh?" retorted

173

the stout woman with the three children. "We make a fine living there, and a lovelier place you couldn't find!"

"Well, as to that, there ain't no accounting for tastes," returned Randy reasonably. "Must see, however, it ain't the place for this young lady."

"Well, I don't see that at all," argued the woman.

"No? But how could you with three brats jumping around you all the time?" returned Randy amiably.

She took offense. "Brats?" she shouted and looked as though she meant to attack.

"Denise . . . come away, do, before Randy and that woman come to fisticuffs," begged Mary on a laugh.

Denise had no choice. She descended the steps and was led away by her friends, and the coach was allowed to continue on its route.

"Now . . . where did you get the money for the ticket?" asked Mary, for she did not see Denise's locket around her neck.

"I . . . I managed," answered Denise. Her cheeks were beet-red.

"Why?" This from Richard. "Have we done something to hurt you?"

"No . . . oh no . . . how could you think that?" She was abashed that her behavior had allowed this thought.

"Why then could you not trust us?" pursued Richard. "Why not tell us in advance this is what you wanted?"

"Because you would not have allowed me to go."

"Right," agreed Richard, grinning, and gave her shoulders a squeeze. "Dennie . . . Dennie . . . how could we let you go?"

Quietly, "There is no reason why you should not."

"I tell you what it is, Richard. Take us home . . . where Dennie and I might be comfortable," said Mary.

"Done!" said Richard, ushering them back into the waiting hack.

"You know," said Randall, coming out of his meanderings, "don't think you can have considered, Denise . . . I mean, really, devilish place, Farnbourgh."

Once at home and alone, Mary went about the business of assuring Denise that she was not pining for Richard. However, Denise found this doubtful. Richard was, after all, in her opinion very close to a god.

There was the fact too that while Mary exerted herself to persecute Denise until the girl confessed she had sold her locket, and had this bought back and returned to Denise, she made no other effort to leave her seclusion behind.

Mary still kept to her room most of the time, did with little to eat and seemed very greatly depressed.

This was to change, however, for Mary's self-imposed confinement lasted only three days before she began to talk herself out of her melancholy.

A rushing emotion very near to violence shook her as she contemplated her life. "Deuce take you for a fool, Mary," she said to her mirrored image. "What the blazes do you mean, hiding yourself away from everyone? Are you afraid to meet him?"

Yes, answered a small voice, Severn . . . you are pining for Severn.

"No, I am not," she answered. "Severn is another woman's lover. He will be father to that woman's child. I care not for such a man."

Well then, retorted the voice, up and out, girl. Do you hear the commotion in the streets outside? This is London. This is your season, and you are a Montlaine!

So it was that Mary's youth and natural optimistic disposition brought her back to her world. However, there was a change in her. She seemed older, less spontaneous with her smiles, and her laughter no longer bubbled as before.

They were promised to the Seftons for a buffet dinner at which there would be a large and merry gathering. Many of Mary's friends and beaux would be there, and she should have looked more in spirits. Instead her cheeks were pale, her eyes lacked their habitual luster, and she seemed lost to other realms. Lady Grey watched her anxiously. Perhaps the evening would bring her out of her doldrums. Perhaps.

Severn came to the Sefton dinner with but one hope, that Mary would be there and ready to receive his apology. He moved about the room, conversed with friends, listened or appeared to listen to lively conversation, but all his movements were underlined with tension. He looked toward the drawing-room doors, for he could hear the bustle of new arrivals. The last three days had used him sternly. He missed his Mary, longed for her, needed her. Nothing seemed quite the same any more, and he wondered how ever he had enjoyed himself before her entrance into his world.

His eyes, when they found her at last, caressed. She looked a sweetheart in the bright-green velvet gown she wore, and then he found her expression and it struck him to the heart. Something was changed here. What was it? What was wrong? His Mary was a fighter, but the girl who walked in here looked defeated, withdrawn and far too pale.

Fiend seize his soul, he thought viciously. Had she been ill? Had he been playing games with her ill at home? He had made no further attempt to contact her after her rejection. He had thought to give her time. . . . He made his way purposefully toward her.

She saw him at once. Oh, he stood out in the mass of the crowd. Tall, broad . . . russet hair flowing about his rugged handsome face. He wore silver-gray velvet over a waistcoat of silver threaded with black. His neckcloth was tied to perfection. His gray velvet pantaloons were neat and uncreased. She discovered his gray eyes, and they glinted but oh so warmly at her. She felt his scrutiny, and she trembled. She should turn away . . . run from him . . . but she could not. She stood riveted, waiting. She knew that he was coming to her and yet she stood.

Pride . . . pride? It deserted her, but she recalled

it and it only served to leave her quivering. She noted through all this that he wore gray . . . silver gray . . . like his eyes . . . like his mistress's favorite gown. That awoke her senses and brought a militant sparkle to her dark eyes.

And then he was there, whispering her name, and all she knew was that it thrilled her beyond comprehension, beyond understanding.

Nina Clifford saw Richard's entrance. She saw her niece standing beside him, and she could have stamped her foot with vexation. It was the outside of enough. He was humiliating her in public. He and his family were supporting her niece when she had refused to do so. He had lied to her. He had said he would return Denise to her uncle, and then suddenly Denise was to be seen everywhere with him.

She was losing him. He had come to call, but she had been out on both occasions. She should make a push to win him back. Why did she not? There was all that family fortune . . . there was the name . . . she would be Lady Grey one day. She moved across the floor, gliding gracefully toward him .

Richard looked up and saw Nina Clifford. Her gold hair brightly wound in a becoming braid at the top of her head. Her gold silk gown clinging seductively to her tall and shapely body. Not long ago he would have been sent into transports over the vision. He was now stirred to admiration, but nothing more, and with something of a start this realization hit him soundly in the face!

Lady Grey was not backward at this junction. She had seen Nina Clifford and correctly interpreted the woman's purpose. Gently and unobtrusively she took Denise's hand.

"Come, child, there is someone I want you to meet."

Richard frowned, for he understood what his mother was at. "But Denise has promised me this waltz." It was a mild objection with no conviction.

"Yes, dear, but I see Mrs. Clifford coming, and she appears to want a word with you . . . besides, it would be more comfortable for Denise to be out of her way." Lady Grey thought herself quite cunning, for this had the desired effect and gave her a neat result.

Richard's chin went up. "Mrs. Clifford may want a word with me, but a waltz is starting and Denise has accepted to allow me to lead her out. As to the rest, Denise has naught to fear from her aunt. Really, Mother, I am surprised that you of all people would sanction such a thing. Run and hide? No, I think not."

Mrs. Clifford was upon them. She greeted Lady Grey cordially, glanced over her niece without a word and turned her full attention on Richard. To him she gave a melting smile and a soft voice.

"Richard? I am so sorry I was not in when you called the other day."

Denise looked away, for her aunt had openly slighted her, and she took it with a tinge of pain. It was hard accepting that she had no one who cared. Here was her mother's younger sister and she cared not a jot for her.

Richard stepped back and brought Denise into full view. "I am sorry," he said in an exaggerated tone, "I must have been standing quite fully in your line of vision, Mrs. Clifford."

Nina Clifford's blue eyes hardened. She stared at him a moment before inclining her head toward Denise.

"Good evening, Aunt Nina," said Miss Avery on a shrinking note.

"Now . . . if you will excuse me?" said Richard quickly, for he could see Nina was about to give her niece a set-down. "Miss Avery has promised me this dance." With which he led Miss Avery off.

Nina Clifford could scarcely control herself. Rage engulfed her, and she took up her silks with a flounce and stamped off. It was the first time any man had taken the reins. It was a new and most humiliating experience. Here was this boy, younger than herself, whom she did not love, and *he* was yanking out of her grasp? It was impossible. Somehow she had made a serious mistake, underrated him.

Denise looked into Richard's face and sighed. "Oh, Richard, I am so sorry . . ."

His countenance relaxed. "Are you? Why?"

"Mary said . . . that you were attached to my aunt."

"Did Mary say that? Well, bright as our Mary is, she is not always correct. What I felt . . . and I did feel strongly . . . has come into focus. . . ."

"But it is all my fault," she wailed.

"Denise, don't you realize . . . 'tis you who have brought me to my senses." He was looking deep into her eyes.

She blushed hotly. What was he saying? No. This was wrong. It was Mary, not she. "Richard . . . it is Mary . . . Mary is the one who has wanted you to draw away from my aunt. Though if I hadn't been in the way . . ."

"What Mary wanted was not to the purpose, Denise . . . and you were not in the way. Oh, to be sure, when I saw Nina react to you . . . I realized that I had created a personality around a beautuful face. The Nina I had designed did not exist . . . but, Denise, you do, and . . . and you matter to me in a way that Nina never did."

"No, no, do not say so. It is all wrong . . ."

"Why? My dearest . . ."

"Don't call me that!" she cut him off. "Don't you realize . . . I am Mary's friend and Mary . . . Mary loves you!"

"Of course she loves me. I love her. What nonsense is this?"

"You don't understand . . . she *loves* you!"

He looked thunderstruck. "Poppycock!"

" 'Tis true. I think she has been pining about it these last days. I think that is why she has been so withdrawn. . . ."

"But Denise . . ."

"No! I will not be the one to hurt Mary." Tears welled in her eyes. "She is my friend. She would just step aside . . . and always I would know."

He thought about it. Mary . . . in love with

him? It could be true. As a girl she had always hero-worshiped him, followed him about, adored him, and he had liked it very well . . . but . . . pine for him? It was impossible . . . or was it? "It cannot be true, Denise. You must be wrong . . . but don't think I don't care, for I do, and I promise I shall not hurt Mary."

Mary was at that moment attempting to cool her blood and still her throbbing heart, which beat irregularly for the tall russet-haired man attempting to sweep her away. "Leave me alone, Severn." It was scarcely audible.

He was alive again. She was here, so very close, and all feelings were centered around her. "I can't, Mary . . . sweet Mary . . . there are so many things I must tell you."

Oh! He was despicable. He was actually making love to her. Yes, he was attempting to seduce her with his wondrous smile, his twinkling gray eyes, his hypnotic voice. Who was here to save her? She looked around, but Denise was dancing with Richard and Lady Grey had gone off. She stood just inside the drawing-room doors in a cavity of space and time where she found herself alone with Severn. It was bliss and it was marbled with pain.

"I don't want to hear anything you may want to say to me. There is nothing that you can say. Please, Severn . . ." Why was she begging? She was a fighter . . . and here she was pleading for mercy. She should have cut him up cold.

He frowned. Why were her eyes filled with

182

sadness? This was not his rebellious spitfire. This was not his hoydenish chit outrageously flaunting her lively spirits. Had the incident at the Dorchester ball done all this? No. "Mary . . . allow me the opportunity to apologize."

He would say sorry and then leave her in peace. Very well, then.

"Your apology is accepted." She inclined her head. "Now, if you don't mind, I think I shall go and visit with . . ."

"But I do mind," he cut her off. "Mary, we are going to talk whether you like it or not." His hand already had her bare arm; he was turning her back to the drawing-room doors.

"What the deuce do you think you are doing?" she breathed on a shocked note.

"Quietly, now . . . for mark me well, I don't give a fig for ought but having a serious talk with you. You, on the other hand, may wish to spare Lady Grey and your friends cause for concern. Therefore, Mary, it behooves you to grant me a few moments of your time. . . ." He was leading her out, down the narrow hall.

"You . . . you churlish boor!" she hissed, quite in a rage now. He was beyond everything a scoundrel. He was right, though . . . she couldn't break out of his hold without causing a scene, and that she would not do. They had reached the library door. He opened it, pushed her gently within and closed the door behind him.

She rounded on him. "Beast! How dare you abduct me in this manner?"

He spread out his hands. "Forgive me, my love

. . . passion lacks ethics." There was a tease in his voice.

Bitterly she threw at him, "You have a great deal of passion, sir, and no ethics at all, so I must concur with your observation!"

Again he frowned and moved toward her. She stepped back.

"Come near me and I *shall* create a scene. That I will not allow, Severn, you may depend on it."

He stood rigid. "Mary . . . I realize I have upset you. I realize I behaved the cad the other night, and I am heartily sorry for it."

"The other night . . . ah, yes, I was nearly forgetting. I should have realized that night what you were . . . but I was stupid enough to think I had done something to make you behave so horribly. I know better now."

This was eye-opening. What was she talking about? What had he missed here? "Your new disgust of me came after that night?"

She bit her lip, turned away and answered the wall. "Yes."

"But Mary . . . you were home ill the next night."

"So I was."

"Well, then . . . how could I have done anything to cause you to reject me now?"

She took a long breath. "Severn, I am not asking you to give me explanations for your way of life. It is your life."

"Mary . . . I want to share it with you." He was upon her, had her shoulders in his grip.

This was back-breaking! Her knees wanted to crumble. She wanted to dive into his arms. She wanted to cry with joy, sing of glory, she wanted to shout her love for him, but Francine's face swam before her eyes. Francine's words came skipping into her ears, blotting out all else. He had his mistress, he would soon have his child, and yet here he stood asking her to share his life.

She yanked out of his hold. "You share your life too freely and with too many. I was not made for such as you!" With this she ran from the room and left him in a sea of misery at her back.

Chapter Fifteen

Mary found Richard. He was her friend. She had so often turned to him in the past. He had been there, her savior during her brother's trials in those horrendous days back in Cornwall. Richard, who for so long she had loved. Richard, who she had for so long believed was the only man she wished to marry.

She reached his side and took up his hand. "Richard . . . ?"

He discovered her eyes. "Mary . . . ? Lord, girl . . . what is it?"

"I . . . I just need you to be near . . . and please keep Severn away from me."

Richard's brows came together, and he growled, "What has the fiend done to you?"

"He is not a fiend . . . and he has not done anything to me . . . I just don't desire his company."

He took Mary's shoulders. "Mary . . . has he . . . has he behaved improperly toward you?"

"No. Please, Richard . . . would you make my excuses to Lady Sefton and see me home?"

He hesitated. There was Denise to think about . . . . he could leave her to Randy's care, for his cousin had just arrived. Yes, he rather thought that was what he would do, for he meant to have a talk with Mary.

Severn returned to the drawing room in time to find Mary rushing into Richard's hold. He saw them in close conversation, and then he saw them some moments later leave together. His world was turning upside down. Mary had rejected him.

Over and over again the thought came back to torture him. Mary had rejected him. This possibility had never occurred to him. When he had made up his mind to have her, when the dawning came through that he loved Mary of Montlaine, it also followed through that he would have her. Somehow he made it through the evening at the Sefton dinner. Somehow he found his way home, found his wing chair and sat by his fire, alone with his thoughts. He would besiege her. He would not stop until she was his!

What had she meant? She had said he shared his life with too many . . . too freely. Just what had she meant? What had stirred Mary into this new fit? How had she come to her conclusion? Someone must have told a tale or two about his style of living . . . but admittedly he had been no monk. That was before her, though . . . why would she object?

Richard took her hand and helped her out of

the hack. "Come on now, girl. You and I are going to have a long talk."

She had refused to converse with him on the ride home. She turned to him now, her resolution on her face. "No, Richard. Keep the hack, return to the dinner party and assure your mother and Denise that all is well with me. They will be fretting over my departure so early in the evening."

"Yes, and with good cause! No, Mary . . . you go on up to the house, I'll just pay off the driver. . . ." He turned away from her and made his way to the little man sitting atop the carriage.

Tom Lewis stood in the shadows. He had been watching the Greys' town house for three days with little sign of Mary . . . until this night. He had seen her go out earlier, and he had stayed on the grounds hidden in the bushes awaiting her return. He didn't know why, for there was no way he would be able to snatch her and be gone with all her people in attendance. Still, he waited, and now he was rewarded for his efforts. He watched her walk up the paved path to the steps. He could see Richard at the curb with the hack. Mary was so near . . . but she was getting away . . . and there was Richard . . . Richard of Grey . . . damn, but it wouldn't be this night. And then a series of events took place, and in the flash of a moment everything changed.

Richard paid off the hack and had turned to follow Mary when he noticed an odd equipage standing near the curbing not far away. He moved

189

toward it with the idea of inspecting it. The horse was old and weathered and was secured to the curbing post by his leathers. The wagon he drew was rotted and empty. Richard's brow went up. What the deuce was such a thing doing here . . . so near his parents' town house?

Mary had put one neat little foot on the first step when one of the household cats scooted out of the bushes, scampered over her foot and vanished once again on the other side of the courtyard garden.

"Pansy!" called Mary. "What are you doing out so late? Come on, you sly little thing . . . come here . . ." With which she turned and followed, intending only to bring in the wayward pet.

Tom held his breath. This was all new to him. It was exciting and repulsive all in one. She was so near . . . Richard was out of sight. Perhaps he had taken the hack home? She was here . . . alone . . . this was his opportunity. His hand reached out, and in the loss of a moment he had her fiercely in his grip!

His hand covered her mouth before he yanked her back against his chest, before he dared to drag her backward into the dark night, away from the torches of the front steps.

Mary felt a hand come out of nowhere and press painfully against her lips. She wanted to cry out with alarm, but the pressure on her mouth and nose made it difficult even to breathe. She was terrified.

Richard? Where was Richard? He would come and save her from this blackguard. What was happening? Who was this horrible man? What did he want? Her beating heart nearly exploded with fear as she struggled against her captor's hold.

Tom Lewis reacted strangely to her struggle. No gentle wench was this. She fought like a crazed tigress. Her silk-shod feet kicked at his ankles. Her fingers clawed at his hands, her body twisted wildly. He must do something. How would he stuff her into the burlap coverings he had provided? He took one of her hands and bent it back, back so that her arm was twisted painfully against her own spine.

He found it served, for she stiffened immediately and gave up the fight. With a satisfied grunt he hissed, "That's it, missie . . . I won't hurt ye if ye behave . . . hold, now . . ." He pulled off the belcher scarf around his neck and whipped the air with it as he brought it to her mouth.

It wasn't easy to manage the thing one-handed. Of necessity his grip slackened, and in that moment she pushed back against him, throwing him off balance. It was then that she managed to scream, *"Richard!"*

It was all over. All considerations were flung aside, for now his life was in jeopardy. Down came the pistol handle on her head, and Mary was knocked unconscious. Quickly he stuffed her into the burlap bag he had provided against the brick wall. A moment later he had lifted her weight to its ledge, scaled its height, slumped her over his shoulder and like a sack of flour laid her in the old wagon waiting for just this cargo!

Richard had decided that while the wagon did not belong at this hour standing so near his parents' residence, it appeared to be harmless. He proceeded to follow Mary up the walk, where he noted there was no sign of her. Odd . . . why did not Tootles still have the door opened for his arrival? Then out of the blackness of the house's flanking courtyard came a terrified shriek.

"Richard!"

He stopped dead. "Mary?" No answer was forthcoming. "Confound it, girl, this is no time to be playing at your games. Mary?"

He moved toward the direction her voice had come from. Why had she screamed like that? What was wrong, and why the devil had she gone for a late-night stroll in the dark? "I say, Mary?"

For no reason at all a chill swept over his spine. For no reason at all his steps quickened. "Mary?" He moved deeper and deeper into the darkness, and his call now was frantic. *"Mary!"*

He reached the far wall, where he heard the scraping of wheels on cobblestone. It resonated in the quiet of the night. He looked over the brick wall and saw a man slumped over the ribbons of the wagon he had investigated. Only this time the wagon was not empty. A dark shapeless bag lay slumped in the wagon's heart. Richard frowned. It had naught to do with him . . . with Mary . . . but then where was Mary? He watched the wagon turn the corner and then suddenly he was sure. He didn't know why. He didn't know what this could mean, but of one thing he was certain . . . that wagon held Mary of Montlaine!

Over the wall he vaulted, down the street he ran on foot. The wagon was just out of sight. Damn, but he would catch up to it, rescue Mary and send the devil that dared this trick to the flames before this night was through!

Morning and chaos descended on the Greys' household. Lady Grey stood in her blue morning gown clasping and unclasping her hands. Her husband had departed on business that morning quite early and would not be back until the following day. Who could she turn to? Denise was as perplexed and worried as she.

Mary was missing. She was not in her room. Her bed had not been slept in. No one had seen her. Randall of Southvale had been dispatched to Richard's lodgings. Richard had seen her home. They must get to the bottom of this.

If this was not enough to vex our lady, a morning caller appeared on the scene to further complicate matters. Tootles stood at the doorway.

"I am very sorry, m'lady. I have advised his lordship that you are overset with a family matter and are not seeing visitors, but he insists . . ."

"Thank you, Tootles," said Lord Severn as he imperiously swept past the butler and entered the room. In one swift glance he could see Denise and Lady Grey looked much agitated. He made Lady Grey a perfunctory bow. "I would not intrude if it were not imperative that I speak with Mary."

Lady Grey withdrew her hand and said in a cool voice, "That is not possible, my lord, and while I do not wish to be rude . . . I must ask you to go. Something . . . of a family nature has come up and needs our . . ."

"He is not there!" cried Randall of Southvale, entering the room unceremoniously. The fact that Lord Severn seemed present did not serve to curb his tongue, for he simply assumed that his lordship was in his aunt's confidence. "Richard never came in last night, Aunt . . . nor has he sent word to his people." He shook his head in some dejection. "I'll tell you what it is. He has run off with her. Stolen her from under my nose!"

Denise so forgot herself as to cry, "No . . . Randall, that cannot be!"

Lady Grey dismissed this as ludicrous. "Why on earth, Randy, should he feel it necessary to run off with Mary when there was not an objection in the world to their making a match of it?" She continued to pace.

Severn recovered his shock, his fear. Of course Mary had not run off with Richard. Her ladyship was correct. Mary would not do such a thing. There was no reason for it . . . was there? He collected himself and said in a grave voice, "I take it that both Mary and Richard are missing?"

Lady Grey turned on him. "My lord . . . what you have heard was not meant for ears outside the family. I trust you will treat it as a confidence."

"Your trust, my lady, is not misplaced. Now . . . is it not possible that Mary and Richard have gone out riding this morning? They were often in this habit, were they not?"

"I wish it might be so ... but one of our servants saw Richard paying off the hack he hired last night ... he naturally assumed that Tootles let them in and proceeded to go about his business. This morning we discovered that Mary's bed had not been slept in, and the gown she was wearing last evening is not among her things."

Severn's heart felt painful pressure. "Then we must assume that something deterred them from entering the house." He was not asking a question but making a statement. He turned away from the assembled group and moved to a window. He turned again to Lady Grey. "Let me try to unravel something ... perhaps it will help. Would you say that Mary has been acting unlike herself since the night of the Dorchester ball?"

In some surprise Lady Grey responded, "Why ... yes."

"Would you kindly tell me ... the morning after the ball ... was it then that she began confining herself to the house?"

"No ... we had an appointment at Madame Burton's."

"Madame Burton's?" Severn's voice was sharp.

"Yes. Mary went in without me ... I went next door. When I arrived at Madame Burton's, Mary had gone home, leaving me the message that she was unwell."

"Who was there, Lady Grey?" His eyes were ice, his voice was hard.

"Why ... no one."

"There was no one there when you arrived? Had no one been in the shop when Mary was there?"

Lady Grey's eyes met Severn's. She knew that Francine White had been his mistress. She also knew the rumor was that he had long since forsaken her. Why had she never put it together? Miss White had been there . . . Madame Burton had mentioned that she was sorry for it but that Miss Montlaine had been in conversation with the Vauxhall singer. She had apologized, for Lady Grey was an important customer and she knew that the quality would not want their flowers associating with such as Miss White.

"I don't know exactly what this has to do with Mary's disappearance, my lord . . . but it was mentioned to me at the time that Miss White had been for a few moments . . . having a chat with Mary." Lady Grey watched him speculatively.

He was spared from comment, though he gritted his teeth, for at that moment Tootles appeared, and this time he brought on the silver salver a sealed envelope addressed to Lady Grey. *It was written in Mary's hand.*

Chapter Sixteen

Lady Grey knew it was Mary's hand the moment she saw it. Mary had a style with a pen that was all her own. Nervously, hopefully, she took the envelope, dismissed Tootles and released a pent-up sigh.

Severn, his hands knotted behind his back, stood patiently awaiting her pleasure while Denise and Randall crowded round her. She ripped open the envelope and unfolded the paper within, putting it up to the light. She read out loud:

My dearest ma'am,

My head aches dreadfully this morning but my jailer tells me it was quite my own fault. You see he had no choice but to knock me out when I chose to struggle and scream. However, rest easy. All is not what it seems. He assures me that he is not a bad man, that he does this for love of a woman and that we have only to comply with their wishes to have me safely returned to you.

It is all very romantic, really, and perhaps one day when this is behind me I shall compose a ballad of this adventure and sing it, but la, Severn alone knows I can't sing.

I am so sorry to cut this short, but I am being told to get to the matter at hand. My jailer wants thirty thousand pounds from you, my beloved brother Montlaine or Severn, whose name he tells me has been linked with mine in song. However, Severn alone must be the man to deliver the money. He is to take the Charing Cross Road south with the money in hand today at three o'clock and he is to travel it unguarded until they choose to relieve him of his burden.

When they have the money safely in hand they will arrange to have me set free.

Yours always,
Mary

Lady Grey read this and came very near for the first time in many years to fainting. She did in fact release something of a wail before Denise took her to the sofa and began the necessary process of comforting her. Randall saw red. He snatched up the letter and announced that he would run the villains through.

Severn composed himself. Mary was in danger. His Mary. No! He would not allow it. He must use all the faculties he had to see her home . . . back to him. He put out his hand toward Randall.

"If I may, sir?"

Randy eyed him, shoved the letter at him and

stalked off toward the sideboard, where he poured his aunt a cup of tea and laced it with brandy.

Severn took the letter to a corner of the room. His insides were tight. His head was reeling. His name had been mentioned often enough in this epistle. That was odd. What had these ruffians in mind? Why was he the one to bring the money? He reread the letter. His brows drew together over his silver-hard eyes. What was this about singing? What did she mean that he knew she couldn't sing? Why did her captor seem to think that she and he were making a match of it? How would a ruffian know such a thing unless he was linked to . . . to someone of their own class?

Mary was pointing a finger. He knew it, felt it and could not find the direction. He was frustrated by it and in no mood for Randy's quip.

"Doesn't make sense," said Randy, shaking his head.

"What doesn't?" asked Severn hopefully.

"Says you know she can't sing. Mary has a pretty little voice. Likes to sing when we go on picnics and outings . . . ever heard her, Severn?"

Severn shook his head impatiently. What was this fool blabbering about? "No, no I never . . ."

"Right then. Answer me this: why does she say *you* know she can't sing?" demanded Randy, triumphantly making his point.

Severn stopped and stared at him. The lad was right, of course. What did it mean? Mary was giving them a clue. Why could they not fathom its meaning?

Randy shook his head. "Poor Mary . . . that

knock on the head . . . could be she is . . ."

"No, Mary is fine . . . just fine. She means something by this, I'll swear," returned Severn.

"Richard?" suddenly screamed Lady Grey. "What have those scoundrels done with Richard?"

Randy went to her and laid his hand on her shoulder. "There, there, aunt. Mary says nothing of Richard . . . don't think they did a thing to him."

"Then where is he? Oh, they have killed my Richard."

Severn shook his head. "No, I don't think so. She says that her jailer is not a bad man . . . I don't think she was trying to set our minds at rest, I think she was attempting to convey a message. I rather think Richard must have heard her scream last night . . . she says that she did. They must have taken her before she reached the front door . . . somehow she and Richard were separated. He is no doubt hot in pursuit."

"Oh, do you think so?" cried Lady Grey hopefully.

Severn nodded and began pacing. Mary was giving him a message. It was meant for him. She knew that Lady Grey would get in touch with him to deliver the money. She knew then that eventually he would read this missive . . . and she was centering her clue around him!

Just what did she mean about a ballad . . . about singing? Why did he not see what she so clearly outlined?

"Nothing has gone right since the Dorchester

all," wailed Lady Grey. "Now what am I to do? Montlaine is in Cornwall and could not be reached before three days' time . . . and my lord is away on business. . . . Severn, how are we to appease these scoundrels by this afternoon?"

Severn was frowning. The money was no great matter. It was Mary's well-being he was concerned about. Her jailers had to be desperate people, for they had abducted her from her own grounds. He could not rely on their word. He could not be certain they would set her free after they had the money in hand. More often than not these things ended badly. Damnation! How could he bear it if Mary came to harm?

Mary was spelling out a message for him alone. Mary believed he would understand. Why could he not? What ingredient had he missed? He took up the letter and again attempted to fathom its clue.

Richard stood at the edge of the woods watching the abandoned cottage anxiously. He was tired. His clothes were damp with the dew of early morning, for he had spent part of the night in the brush. He had followed the wagon until his legs would carry him no more. He then spotted a trademan's nag loosely in tow. He took out one of his cards, shoved it into the startled merchant's hand and called out as he took the lead of the horse's halter, "I need your animal, sir, 'tis a matter of life and death. Contact me for compensation!" With this he had hopped onto the horse's bare back and without the benefit of a bridle or saddle he took up the halter leading rope and spanked the old nag into action. It loped off amiably enough, but the wagon was already out of sight. An inquiry here, another there, put him in the right direction. However, he never again caught sight of the wagon that night.

Determinedly and with every effort bent on discovering his quarry's direction, Richard was bound. Passersby were few, and even fewer were those willing to aid his hunt. Richard produced a coin whenever he thought it would serve and discovered that a wagon carrying a single load, driven by a man, had taken the South Road out of London.

There was no moon, and stars were obscured by clouds. It was not easy going, and the nag beneath his weight stumbled often. With London behind him, he had finally given up hope. He would find shelter and begin his search from this point at dawn. Securing his horse, he dragged himself to a fir tree, removed his velvet coat and laid himself down, pulling his coat over him like a blanket. He was exhausted, for he had been at it for hours, and sleep came.

It seemed that he had scarcely dozed off when he was awake again, and in truth this was so, for he had been asleep only two hours before dawn came and shook him to action. He awoke with a start, unsure of his surroundings, unsure how he happened to be there. Then it all flooded back. Mary. Someone had run off with Mary.

He brushed off the pine needles, donned his velvet cutaway somewhat worse for wear and undid his nag's lead. Nimbly he hopped back onto the animal's back and led him to the road. He backtracked. Instinct moved him, chance directed, and he found that last night he had missed a fork in the road!

He veered off onto the country dirt road, and after two miles of going discovered to his excitement an abandoned cottage in the clearing just ahead. He slid off the horse and swiftly made for the trees. This was the place . . . for there at the cottage's rear dilapidated barn was the old cob horse and weathered wagon. Its cargo was gone.

Richard of Grey could have cursed himself out loud. He had no weapon on him. In his haste he had not armed himself. Fool! He looked about and found a large handy branch and took it up before he began stalking the cottage.

Suddenly he was diving into the bush, for there was a single rider coming toward the cottage. She was wearing an elegant riding habit. Her blond hair was drawn silkily away from her face. *Here was Francine White.*

Was he going mad? Had he followed the wrong scent? What to do? Wait, Richard . . . wait for the outcome. A dark-haired man some ten years older than himself came out of the cottage and pulled her off the horse and into his arms . . . and then the two were reentering the cottage.

He waited. What was this? Just what was this? Francine White and a gypsy, for the unshaven man looked no more than that. Was he at the wrong place? Could he have been wrong about the wagon . . . the horse?

Mary's feet were tied, as were her hands. She could hardly breathe, for he had stuffed a gag into her mouth. He had come in earlier and untied her hands.

"Here," he said, shoving paper and quill at her. "Yer to write a ransom letter. 'Tis the only way ye will be set free."

She indicated that she wished to have the gag removed. He sighed but complied.

Carefully she said, "I will write this letter, sir, if you allow me to assure my people that I am well. I don't want them unnecessarily frightened." She had a plan. Earlier that morning she had heard him sending for someone. She had heard him in the other room directing a young person (who sounded like a boy) to take a message to Francine White's lodings in London. It all made sense, for he had apologized to her when she had come to. He had said he hadn't wanted to hurt her, hadn't wanted to abduct her, but he and his lady . . . well, they had to get away.

At first she had had to digest this. Francine White and this man? But Francine was Severn's mistress . . . carrying Severn's child. Or was she?

He considered her request. "Aye . . . ye can write yer people ye be in good hands . . . tell 'em I mean ye no harm if I can help it . . . but tell 'em we want thirty thousand pounds . . . tell 'em only Severn is to deliver it and tell 'em that he is to take the Charing Cross Road this afternoon at three o'clock."

"How will you get the money from him?"

"Never ye mind. Tell them that Severn is to ride with the money alone. We'll take it when we sees fit."

"Will you then set me free?"

"Aye . . . when we knows we are safe enough."

She composed her letter. Purposely, anxiously lest the man catch on, she put in the remark about the ballad, her singing . . . she directed her remarks toward Severn.

This done he bound her, gagged her and shoved her back into a corner. She waited for the door to close behind him. She wobbled herself until she was up on her knees. She raised her arms to the rusty nail she found sticking out of a worn beam and she began working at the linen holding her hands.

Gleefully Francine went into Tom's arms. "You've done it. My Tom, you are like no other. Now Severn will deliver the money and we shall be on our way. . . ."

"I won't ever do anything like this again, Francie. It has made me fairly sick. The way that little missie looks at me . . . like I am some kind of monster ready to pounce on her . . ."

"Never mind her. Give me her letter. I shall take it back to London immediately and have it delivered."

"You'll pack . . . be ready, love. I want you waiting for me in Dover by evening."

"I'll be there, Tom." She took the note, and he led her outside again and helped her to mount her steed.

Richard watched her as she headed back to London. Now, why the devil should Francine White take a two-hour ride out of London, spend five minutes with this man and then head back to London? He began creeping up on the house.

Mary tore through. Her wrists were bloody from the effort, as the nail had scraped her skin as well as the material. She yanked off the gag and began working the ties at her ankles. All at once there was a war going on in the other room.

Richard had exploded into the cottage and demanded roughly, his stick raised into the air, "Where the devil do you have Mary?"

Tom was startled into stupidity, but made a recovery, whereupon he lunged not toward Richard but away, and when he brought himself up he had a gun leveled.

Richard made a growling sound and threw his bat. Tom reacted by pulling the trigger, and Mary flung open the door in time to see Richard falling to his knees!

"No!" she screamed and went to Richard.

He smiled sheepishly. "Well, Mary . . . I've found you. Made something of a mull out of it, though."

"You are wonderful, Richard. Imagine your finding me! Now, where has he caught you?" she said, going to her knees and finding that Tom's bullet had skimmed through Richard's thigh. It had taken a large chunk of flesh with it when it went, but it had not lodged itself.

"Oh, Richard . . . it is very nasty and will need immediate attention if it is not to fester." She turned to Tom. "You said you are not a bad man. Very well, you may not have been, but you are fast changing the fact, are you not? Is this also for love?"

"Lookee . . . I was only defending myself."

"Against what? You had a gun . . . did he?"

"No, but . . ."

"Get us something to clean this wound. Alcohol will have to do for a time . . . and clean rags."

"I've got some whisky . . . but naught else."

She pulled a face and began tearing at the linen slip she wore beneath her red gown. While she tended Richard's wound, Tom considered this new problem.

"How did ye get loose, missy?"

"There was a nail," she answered simply.

"Ye bloodied yer fine arms," observed Tom. "There was no need. We would have let ye go by tomorrow night."

"I like to come and go as I please," she returned.

"Aye, jest like all yer kind. Now what's to do? I'll have to truss ye both up . . . back to back, more 'n likely, and Lord knows I didn't want to make ye more uncomfortable than I had to."

"Hold just a moment, sir!" demanded Mary. "You will not come near me until I have Richard's wound attended to."

"Aye," agreed Tom unhappily.

Richard sighed as he sat back and allowed Mary to minister to his leg. He winced with pain as she dabbed the wound with whisky. "Confound it, Mary, I have botched up matters, haven't I? No doubt you would have been free and clear if I hadn't taken the place by storm!"

"Nonsense. Where could I have gone on foot? Besides, by now Miss White will soon be in London, and the note Tom had me write will be delivered to your mother."

"Note? What note?"

"Ransom, Richard. Imagine. They think I am worth thirty thousand pounds," she said banteringly.

He grinned. "They have never lived with you."

"Kindly, now, dear, don't want your head shot off too, do you?" she returned sweetly.

He laughed shortly. "So 'tis ransom, and then what?"

"And then we'll be pleased to let ye go," answered Tom.

"Ha!" retorted Richard. "Never say so, for it's a round tale. I ain't green!"

"Ye'll be set free, I tell you!" returned Tom agitatedly.

"No, Tom, you can't really believe that," said Mary. "You could be hanged for this crime, you and your Miss White. We know who you are."

"It don't matter. Francie told me . . . we would go away, change our names," stuck in Tom worriedly.

"No, my friend. You may not have our ends in

your mind, but let me assure you, your lady does," answered Mary.

"No, you're wrong, missy. Francie said she would hire someone to come out here and let you go as soon as we were safely out of reach," argued Tom.

"She would hire someone, but not to release me ... and now Richard. Oh, no," pursued Mary. "You can't really believe that."

"Of course he doesn't believe that," put in Richard in disgust. "He has just chosen to look the other way!"

"Stubble it! I don't want to hear any more," raged Tom as he made for them, linens and ropes in hand.

Chapter Seventeen

Francine White went immediately after arranging the letter's delivery to hire a post chaise and four. This done, she proceeded to her lodgings, where she ordered her maid to start packing.

This they did with more speed than tidiness, and it was not long before the driver of the chaise was loading her trunks and she and her maid were making ready for their journey. She would, of course, do as her Tom asked and proceed to Dover. However, there was a stop she would make first.

There was a man she knew who ran a tavern on the South Road. She would stop and make arrangements with him that Tom must never know about. Mary would not be killed . . . oh no, there was no profit in that. No, this tavernkeeper would know just how to turn a pretty sum over with Mary!

She sat back against the leather upholstry of the carriage seat and rewarded her maid with a smile. She had a hefty sum of jewels hidden away, enough fashionable clothes to last her a few months, and soon her Tom would have the money they needed to get started in Paris. Severn would suffer over his pretty little innocent . . . and that was nearly as satisfying as all the rest!

Randall left the bank with assurances that his and Lord Severn's signatures were more than adequate to elicit the sum they required. It would be delivered within the hour. He looked up and saw Miss White's loaded chaise pass by, and his brow went up with surprise. Where was she off to? He knew she was engaged to sing at Vauxhall that very night . . . yet here she was, off . . . and taking the route that led to the South Road. Odd.

In the Greys' drawing room Severn was pacing. Lady Grey was reclining on her sofa, her head beneath her palms, and Denise was organizing her thoughts.

It was all very strange. How had she imagined that Mary was in love with Richard? Was she so blind? Here was Severn, and even a total noddy could see that he was in love with Mary . . . and this fact explained so many things.

Mary had not been pining for Richard. Of course she had not. It was Severn that Mary so often laughed with. It was Severn that Mary had been looking for those days when he had been away. It was Severn that Mary unconsciously quoted so often. And it was Severn's mistress that had sent Mary off to her room where she hid herself away. Why had she not realized this before? What had

Miss White said to Mary to make her pine?

"Excuse me my lord . . ." started Denise carefully. "There is something I should like to have clarified."

"What is it?" asked his lordship testily. He was attempting to discover the clue in Mary's letter. All thoughts were concentrated toward that end.

"Earlier . . . before Mary's letter was brought to us . . . Lady Grey mentioned something about Mary and Francine White meeting one another at Madame Burton's."

"And what bearing does that have on our problem?" demanded his lordship irritably.

She blushed. "Naught, really . . . but Miss White is the singer at Vauxhall . . ."

"Yes, yes . . . do get to the point!" broke in Severn impatiently.

"I wondered if Mary and Miss White had . . . had something of a feminine skirmish during that meeting?"

Lady Grey sat up. Severn stopped his pacing and exchanged glances with Lady Grey. He said carefully, "What makes you ask that?"

She braced herself. "I don't think Mary knew that you were involved with Miss White . . . however, it is possible that Miss White had heard something about Mary's being seen quite a lot in your company."

Again he stood transfixed, digesting this. Very well, he thought, it explained Mary's behavior. She had been shocked by Francine.

"I don't see what that may have to do with what we are now facing."

She sighed. "No . . . but I rather thought your experience with Miss White might allow us to either dismiss her from or admit her to suspicion."

There was no opportunity to answer this, for Randall walked in at that moment and announced, "It's done! They'll have the money here within the hour. Don't like it, Severn. Things are moving too fast . . . and we could end by losing you, losing the money and never finding Mary!"

Denise sighed and caught Severn's attention again. "I have made a very bold suggestion about someone I don't even know . . . it was just that . . . well, Mary's repeated reference to singing and song . . ."

"Eh? And that's another very odd thing. Francine White, you know," said Randy on a note of puzzlement.

All eyes turned to him, and Severn demanded, "What about Francine White?"

"She's off, you know . . . saw her in a post chaise bound for the South Road. Trunks loaded to the hilt . . . and the thing is she is engaged to sing at Vauxhall's tonight."

All thoughts centralized into one. Mary had pointed him in this direction. All her clues had led to this conclusion, and why had he not seen the answer sooner?

He scooped up his hat. "Damnation, man . . . I'll wring her neck!"

"Severn . . . where are you going? You have to deliver the money this afternoon," cried Lady Grey.

"I am going to do much better than that, ma'am. I am going to deliver my Mary safe and sound by nightfall." With this he was gone from the house.

Tom eyed his captives. It was nearly time to leave them. Soon he would sit in waiting for Severn on the Charing Cross Road south. He knew just the spot. His pistol was in his belt. It wouldn't be difficult. Then why was he perspiring over the thought?

He moved to them and undid Mary's gag. "There, missy . . . I'll be giving you a sip of water before I leave. . . ."

"Thank you . . . but you must also attend to Richard," she said softly.

He sighed heavily but did as he was asked. Richard used the opportunity to plead with the man for Mary's release.

"Look, man . . . you have something of a heart . . . let Mary go . . . take her with you for a bit if you have to . . . but you see to it that she is safely released after you have your money."

He eyed Richard. "There's no need, lad . . . the two of ye will be set free soon enough. I told ye . . . Francine has arranged for a local lad to do the thing . . . after we be free and clear."

Mary looked away. "Oh, Tom . . . you are throwing your life away . . . she carries another man's child. Did you know that?"

He gave a short laugh. "Naw . . . she told ye that, missy, to get your bristles up against his lordship. She's got her mean streak, m'Francie . . . but she's got reason enough."

It was impossible talking to the man, and it wasn't long before they were watching him go. They struggled against each other in their attempt to ease the tightness of the ropes that bound them together. It did not serve. They couldn't shout, for he had gagged them again before his departure. However, Mary would not give up. She squirmed, she wriggled, she tore her gown and her flesh, but suddenly she felt one wrist band loosen, and with this incentive she managed to make Richard understand that they must inch their way to the wall where she might use the nail again to their advantage. She never realized during all this effort that his wound began bleeding, that his pain was excruciating and that the dirt of the floor was covering his open laceration!

Francine White rose from the table. Instructions and a sizable sum had been delivered into the hands of the whiskered round-shouldered blackguard seated before her. She had no doubt that he would carry out his deal. He had too much to gain from the sale of an innocent girl to forgo it.

"Trussed up is she now, yer sure?" asked the man again.

"I've already told you, she won't be any trouble, but you must make haste . . . for my . . . my partner will soon have left her, and I don't want to take the chance she might escape."

"A thousand pities yer man didn't deem fit to

give her a brace of laudanum. It would 'ave 'elped matters."

"Just take your barking iron, man, and you won't have any trouble," said Francine on a note of impatience. She was already walking away.

She situated herself in her chaise and gazed languidly at the passing scenery. Her maid chatted incessantly, but for once Francine did not rebuke her. Too good was her mood. And then suddenly she was rudely awakened from her fantasies.

Severn appeared out of nowhere. His dapple-gray gelding was in a total body sweat and snorting for air, as Severn had ridden the poor beast hard. He was yanking open the door, pulling the young maid out, abruptly telling her to climb up with the driver, and then he was seating himself beside Francine.

She found her voice and began to object when the glinting edge of a knife hypnotized her into rigidity. He brought the blade very near to her lovely face.

"Your man has been informed that you are wanted by the runners, that he is not to proceed until I have given him leave. You are, my dear, quite in my hands."

"It is a state I have ever strived for," she said easily. "But Severn . . . you need not . . . threaten me to it."

"Ah, Francine, don't you realize you have an engagement at Vauxhall tonight?"

"I don't care to give it. Severn . . . what does

this mean? Why have you accosted me in this fashion?" Her nerves had begun to react. There was something in his eyes that quite frightened her.

He brought up the glinting blade and eyed it. "What a shame it would be, Francine, if you could no longer perform . . . no longer show your face."

"Severn . . . ?"

"Yes, I must be careful, mustn't I? Don't want this to slip across your pretty cheek."

"Severn. You wouldn't. You are not that sort of man . . ."

"Am I not? But you see, I am a man driven. I am a man in love with a chit of a girl, and Francine . . . it has come to my knowledge that you are the one who has taken her out of my reach!"

"No . . . Severn . . . 'tis a lie . . ."

"Is it?"

"I . . . I don't know what you want . . ."

"Don't you?"

She stared into his hard steel eyes. Quick, she had to think of something to throw him off. "Oh, if you mean that I teased her with a bit of foolery about carrying your child . . ."

His brow went up. He wanted to slap her face. So that was it.

"Damn your soul, Francine!" In more ways than he could tell, this woman had tortured his love. He wanted in that moment to kill, and he wondered fleetingly if he could in fact tear the blade across her face as he was threatening. No, not even now. It was a bluff, but one that he must make work.

She saw danger to herself. He was crazed. "Stop it, Severn . . . do not . . ."

"Then don't play games. I haven't the time. Mary's ransom note as much as spelled it out that you were behind her abduction!"

Francine had not read the letter. She was thunderstruck by this and made a slip. "That fool . . ."

"Yes, he is a fool, for Mary also wrote that he does this deed for love of you." He put this in to convince her that there was no use denying anything now.

She bit her lip. "I . . . don't know anything."

Sure now that she did, he brought the knife to her cheek. "Have it your way, jade!"

She felt the sharp blade prick at her skin and screamed, "Stop it, Severn!"

"Where is Mary?"

"Oh God . . . it might already be too late . . . I don't know if she will still be there."

"What the devil do you mean?" demanded Severn.

"There is a fork in the road some miles back . . . you needs must take it to a country road . . . the fingerpost is worn and the name is not discernible. There is a clearing off that road upon which rests an abandoned cottage. She is in there . . . but Severn . . . 'tis nearly three . . . someone will soon be there to collect her . . ."

He threw her away from himself, for he understood too well her meaning. "You unpardonable jade! Mark me, Francine, if she is not there, if she is harmed, there is nowhere in this world you can hide from me!"

With this he was gone and heading at a reckless pace for his destination. Francine watched for a moment. It was true . . . if Mary was gone already, Severn would hunt her down . . . she had seen it in his eyes. What would she do now?

She had to go on . . . had to meet her Tom . . . who would be waiting on the Charing Cross Road for Severn. He would give it up after a while and he would come to Dover to meet her . . . but then what?

At last, Mary's wrists were free. Her efforts had reopened the minor cuts she had won herself earlier that day when she had managed to release her bonds. Quickly she worked free her gag and then chatted happily enough as she worked her ankles and the ropes that bound her to Richard. Richard, she noticed suddenly, was slumped.

"Richard?" She turned around and discovered that he was unconscious. "Richard?" she screamed somewhat frantically.

His breeches were soaked in blood. She felt his head and found him feverish. Oh God, this day and her struggles to be free had worked him badly. She jumped to her feet and scouted out some water and the jug of whisky. She washed down his wound, made a tourniquet and then began bathing his head. He opened his eyes.

"Eh . . . Mary . . . where . . . ?"

"Hush, Richard. We are still in the cottage, but

we are unguarded. When you are well enough we will leave."

"You leave ... Mary ... it's you that is in danger ..."

"No! Richard ... I think soon someone will come to ... to do away with us ... and you know I can't leave you here. I shall go outside and see if that wagon is still here."

She laid his head down and got to her feet. As she reached for the doorknob it opened toward her and she jumped back to find a large, round-shouldered man with a shock of unkempt hair beneath his woolen cap. He grinned at her and displayed a mouth wanting a great number of teeth.

"Lookee 'ere ... ye got free, did ye, mort?" He reached out for her arm.

Richard managed to sit up and attempted to rise. The man looked surprised to find him there. "Well, well ... she didn't say naught about a flash cull ... but I sees ye be done in, man ... I'll jest be finishing the job ... naught to it, really ..." He pulled out a horse pistol from his waistband.

Mary screamed, "No ... please don't hurt him ... he doesn't know anything. Doesn't know me ... just wandered in by mistake ... please ..."

The man considered this, and Mary found the opportunity to deliver a quick kick to the man's shin. He bent over, and she landed him a blow to his pistol arm with the wooden chair that had been near her side. The pistol skidded across the wooden floor, and the man made a dive for it. Mary too scrambled for it, but the villain caught

221

it up and planted Mary a facer that sent her sprawling backward.

It was the last thing he did before he slumped into unconsciousness. Severn had arrived in time to see his Mary slapped backward, and it was all he could do to keep himself from killing her attacker. His gun butt found its mark, and then he was scooping his Mary into his arms.

She was dazed and her cheek smarted where the man had caught her, but she looked up into Severn's face and smiled. "Well, 'tis about time you got here, my lord!"

In spite of everything that had happened, Severn put his head back and whooped with laughter, and then softly, so softly, said, "My sweet Mary . . ." With which his lips took hers.

After a time Richard coughed. "I wonder if it would be too much trouble to remember that I am bleeding to death on this confounded floor?"

Epilogue

So it was that the innkeeper Francine had hired was secured in the cottage and left for the authorities. Severn also managed to hire a carriage of sorts and convey his Mary and Richard of Grey back to town in some show of comfort.

Tom and Francine were allowed to go on their way, leaving them to their fates as punishment, as Severn wanted not the least breath of scandal to touch his Mary. Francine and Tom did not prosper, but then Francine's needs were against them. Scarcely a month passed before Francine left Tom in Dover and took on Paris. Sadly, he turned and went up north to the coal mines.

However, that same month saw the names of Montlaine and Severn united. Sweetly did Mary lead her lord a dance, and many were the surprised faces, for joyously did he follow.

Richard of Grey too seemed fairly nabbled, and it was whispered that the penniless Denise Avery was the arrow that had taken his heart.

Mary remarked upon it one morning. Her husband sat perusing his newspaper, so very naturally she slid onto his lap, making his efforts more difficult.

"Richard and Dennie will make a match of it soon. . . ."

"Hmmm," remarked her husband.

"That leaves only Randy to take care of," she pursued.

He looked at her. "Leave Randy alone. He can find his own bride."

"I know . . . but the trouble is . . . I think he has found the wrong one, Severn!"

"Leave it alone," retorted her husband anxiously. "Mary . . . he is a full-grown man, capable of making his own decisions."

"Yes, and so was Richard. If I had let it alone, he would have married Nina Clifford and been miserable."

"But Mary . . ."

"If I had left it alone . . . you would never have consented to help me make him jealous, and only look how *that* turned out!"

He chuckled and touched her cheek. "Ah, Mary . . ."

To this she dropped a kiss on his lips, jumped off his lap and clapped her hands together. "I knew you would approve. I shall start on it right away." With this she sprang into action.

Her husband put down his newspaper and started after her, thought better of it and sighed. She was, after all, and would always be his Mary, sweet Mary.